Melanie Franner is a freelance writer who currently lives in Ontario, Canada. She loves to travel, is an avid reader and is fond of being outdoors (especially in the summer!). Over the years, Melanie has written business articles for numerous industry magazines. *Moments in Time* is her first foray into the fictional world.

To Robert Frank Franner—my husband, my mentor, my friend.

Melanie Franner

MOMENTS IN TIME

AUSTIN MACAULEY PUBLISHERS™

LONDON • CAMBRIDGE • NEW YORK • SHARJAH

A CIP catalogue record for this title is available from the British Library.

ISBN 9781788781985 (Paperback)
ISBN 9781788781992 (Hardback)
ISBN 9781788782005 (E-Book)

www.austinmacauley.com

First Published (2018)
Austin Macauley Publishers Ltd™
25 Canada Square
Canary Wharf
London
E14 5LQ

I would like to express my sincere gratitude to my friends and family—especially my mother. Without them, this book would not have been written.

Chapter One

There are 40-odd people in the house. Some of them are family. Okay, a few of them are family. Others are acquaintances, people I've come into contact with over the years. They are all milling about, looking like they are enjoying themselves while trying to inconspicuously steal glances my way. I know they mean well. I realize that they are all genuinely concerned about me—some more than others. But regardless, I want them out of my house. Now.

You see, this house is my sanctuary. It used to be our sanctuary. My husband and I spent over 20 years in this house, slowly molding it into the custom-designed abode that could sustain our need for privacy. We were reclusive in a way. Two peas in a pod driven by our desire to be alone. Some said we were eccentric, whatever that means in this day and age. But we were happy. Really happy.

Until my husband died. Which happened last night.

Even then, we were alone. The emergency-room doctor had pulled me aside. Told me there was no hope. The cancer had taken its toll. He asked if I wanted to call someone, if I wanted someone by my side when I said my final goodbye.

He had no idea that it had always been just the two of us; that there wasn't anyone else with whom I wanted or needed to share this experience. No, it was going to be just the two of us until the very bitter end. And it was.

My husband would have been happy about that. If he had been alive to see it, which of course, he wasn't. That's why I now have all of these people in my house, glancing furtively my way. Meanwhile, I am just desperately trying to hang on.

"How are you doing dear?"

It's my mother. She is already attired in black. Has always been concerned about appearances, although she dresses well below her age. Which is 70. Today, she's wearing a pair of low-slung slacks with a wide gold belt. A form-fitting grey sweater completes the look, along with the gold-hoop earrings of course. She extends a cup of coffee towards me.

"Here. Drink this. You'll feel better."

I take it from her. My mind is on autopilot. The smell alone sends bile rising from my stomach. I know it won't make me feel better. A bottle of wine, on the other hand, might be enough to knock me out for a few hours, which would provide me some relief. But I make no move toward the alcohol table.

My dad is on the ball. One of the first things he did after 'the call' was to come over and set up the table. And it was good thinking on his part, as that's where most of the group has congregated.

A good drinker in his day, my dad recognizes the value of alcohol in emotional situations. That's probably why my mother and he split after a 23-year marriage that produced two siblings, siblings who somehow managed to remain close throughout a very bad break up that pitted the two sides against the other.

"Give me that cup of coffee. Take this instead," my sister advises, handing me a glass of red wine, which she knows is a staple of mine. "Honestly, what is that lady thinking? She's got no idea of what you're going through. I know it's tough. It's going to be a long road out of this but you will get there. And if alcohol helps do the trick, so be it. We can worry about getting you into treatment later."

I crack the beginnings of a smile, amazed that I am capable of such a manoeuver at a time like this. But the tears are threatening to let loose on the tidal wave of emotions coursing through me. I grab the glass, give her the cup of coffee and take a big gulp. And then another.

"Thanks," I mutter. "Just what the doctor ordered."

In fact, the doctor had ordered sleeping pills. And anti-depressants. And a whole mix of other mind-numbing drugs.

Not at the same time but over the last 12 months when my husband's health had begun its final descent. I politely refused them all, determined to experience every painful second of the voyage with my husband. We were, after all, two peas in a pod.

I toss down the rest of the glass and am pleasantly surprised to see another instantly appear. My sister is one of my best friends. I nod appreciatively and slowly begin making my way out of the melee. I may not be able to get these people out of my house, but I can get myself out or, at least, away from this room.

I make a beeline for the bedroom—the only bedroom we have, I might add. Designed intentionally that way so that we wouldn't have to put up with visitors hoping to spend the night. Sure, there had been a couple of exceptions over the years, but this unusual architectural feature had worked well for the most part.

As I enter the room, I am overcome with grief. I fall on the bed and try to stifle the wails that threaten to escape. I have to retain some semblance of composure, at least until these people leave my house. Which is why I want them to go. I am losing that steadfast control that has kept me sane over these past few months. And I don't want anyone around to witness my collapse. I am determined to do this on my own, as a sort of homage to my husband. I need to show him that he was right to rely upon me, to trust me to be his rock. I have been strong enough for the two of us. And I can't let him down now. I close my eyes and beg for sleep, which mercifully arrives.

Chapter Two

My husband and I are in the car, his car to be exact. It's a Sapphire Blue Audi A3. We're cruising along the country roads and enjoying the sights as they whiz by. We're exceedingly happy. Just going out for a Sunday drive to get some fresh air. We've never been to this town but I know before we even make the turn that there will be a Dairy Queen on the next street. I am addicted to Dairy Queen, actually to the company's ice cream Blizzards. And my husband knows this.

"Turn left here," I say. "There's a Dairy Queen around the corner."

My husband looks in my direction and smiles. He knows about this hidden talent of mine. He no longer questions my instincts.

Once, as a surprise, my husband installed an app on my iPhone that would automatically locate the nearest Dairy Queen. I didn't have the heart to tell him that I intuitively knew where they were, or at least where most of them were.

We turn the corner and sure enough, there's the telltale red and white logo. I glance over, a proud smile on my face. I've done it again. But the moment is shattered with an ear-splitting noise. I look to either side of us to see if there is someone blaring the radio in the next car.

And then I realize it's not music playing. It's a vacuum cleaner. And my husband isn't beside me in the car but dead in a hospital morgue. Reality hits hard and I groan in despair, willing sleep to overcome me once again. But it doesn't work this time, and I eventually drag myself out of bed.

My appearance in the living room is greeted by the close-knit family of the night before. Who knows where they all slept or if they even stayed here. There certainly wasn't room in this house. My mother is the one vacuuming, naturally. My dad is pacing in the kitchen, trying to avoid my mother. And my sister is reclining on the couch, reading a magazine. My step-father and step-mother are sitting in facing chairs, looking as awkward as the situation dictates.

There are no signs of my husband's relatives. His sister is the only family remaining and she lives in another province. She knows what has happened, was too upset to come to the phone to hear it herself so had her husband act as the go-between. I could hear her crying in the background. I was stronger than that, able to relay the news without breaking down. But that was last night. This is a new morning.

"Oh, sorry dear, I didn't mean to wake you," says my mother. And I wonder how that can be when she is vacuuming a mere ten feet from where I was sleeping.

"It's okay," I reply. "I guess I needed to get up anyway."

My sister comes over and gives me a hug, which almost loosens the floodgates once again.

"Cup of coffee? Orange juice? A glass of wine?" she asks.

I manage a weak smile and opt for the coffee.

"I guess we'll have to start making some funeral arrangements," states my mother, who looks like she wants to keep vacuuming instead. "Do you want us to take care of it? Of course, you'll use the funeral home in town. We will have to pick out a casket and then there's the service to arrange and the visitations."

"There isn't going to be a service," I reply. "I think we'll just have a memorial later."

My mother knows that my husband is—I guess was—an atheist. I've told her that my Catholic upbringing had long gone by the wayside as well and that he and I were of the same mind when it came to religion. But she chooses to ignore this, as she has chosen to ignore many things in my life.

"Are you sure that's what you want? Don't you think everyone should have a chance to grieve?" she asks.

Truth be told, I don't really care about anyone else. I have a hard enough time dealing with me and my current situation. I've no energy or emotion to spare at the moment.

"We talked about it before he died and decided on cremation and a memorial service," I reply.

I see my sister shoot a quick look at my father. He gets the message and steps up to the plate—all in a matter of seconds.

"I think that's a fine idea," my dad says. "If that's what you two decided, then that's what you should do."

I sit down on the couch, exhausted already.

My husband didn't actually decide that. He said that he didn't give a damn what happened after he died, that I could do whatever I chose. I hadn't wanted to tell either of my parents about that discussion, so opted for the small white lie instead.

"In that case, I am going to cremate you and put your ashes in the kitty litter box," I jokingly said to him one night.

"You do whatever you like," he replied, tickling me into laughter.

My husband had a wicked sense of humour. He could make a deaf man laugh. There were times when we couldn't catch our breath because we were laughing so hard, tears streaming down our cheeks as we gulped for air.

A few weeks before he died, my husband told me that he had changed his mind and that he now wanted me to do something specific with his ashes. I had informed him about my plan to spread them on our country property. I never considered the kitty litter as a serious option.

"I want you to go to Berlin and drop my ashes on the stage of the Berliner Philharmonie," he told me that night. I was dumbstruck. I knew that my husband was a huge classical music fan and that his tastes ran to the Berlin Philharmonic. We had actually flown to Berlin a few times to hear them play.

"Are you serious?" I asked incredulously. This was a far cry from the kitty litter box or even the backyard for that matter. "How the hell am I supposed to do that?"

He never spoke about it again but inside, I became determined to fulfill his last wish.

Chapter Three

My husband was always a joker. And a smart man to boot. I remember the first night that I brought him home to meet my father and step-mother. We were just finishing dinner, complemented by a few glasses of wine, and the two men were talking hockey.

My husband was a die-hard hockey fan. Regardless of how poorly his team played or how hopeless the situation, he would steadfastly keep on cheering and rooting for the win.

One of our first outings together was to attend a hockey game. My father had promised to get me tickets (which were extremely hard to come by). My husband, who was just a 'friend' at the time, had plans to go to the Auto Show earlier that day. We had arranged to meet at a certain time in front of the main doors of the arena. This was in the days before cell phones.

Unfortunately, my dad's tickets didn't come through. I was in a tizzy, picturing my friend waiting for me for hours. Should I go and wait for him? It was a bit of a drive into the city and not one I particularly wanted to make if it was to just turn around and come back. In two cars, no less.

I knew that he was meeting up with his father that afternoon. But I had never spoken to the man; didn't even know if he knew my name.

What to do?

After deliberating frantically for some time, I pulled out the city phone book. How hard could it be?

A couple of wrong numbers later, I finally connected with the right person.

"Hi. I don't know if you know who I am but I'm a friend of your son. We were supposed to meet up tonight for the hockey game because my dad was going to get us a couple of tickets. Well, turns out he couldn't get the tickets, which means, of course, that we can't go to the hockey game. Unless we buy some. But that's pretty expensive. And we'd have to get them from scalpers," I rambled on nervously, not even stopping to catch my breath. "So that's why I am calling you, even though you don't know me. I think you're planning on meeting up with your son at the Auto Show and I was wondering if there is any way you can tell him that I couldn't get the tickets, that I'm really sorry and that I hope he isn't too disappointed?"

There was complete silence on the line for what seemed like two minutes. I was just about to take a deep breath and repeat every painful word all over again when I heard my future father-in-law say:

"No ticky. No laundry."

And he hung up the phone.

I was stunned. I knew that my husband's parents were from Europe—his father from Hungary and his mother from Germany. Could it be that he didn't speak English? That he didn't understand a word I said?

I debated whether to call back and try to explain again. Perhaps I wouldn't ramble on quite so quickly and he could make better sense of my request.

Instead, I opted to spend the next several hours anxiously awaiting news. Was he there at the arena, getting angrier as each minute passed? Was he worried that I had been in a car accident? What could he possibly be thinking?

Turns out his father spoke English very well and managed to convey my message far in advance of any ill effect. It also seems that I am severely lacking when it comes to the use of idioms in the English language. Who'd have 'thunk' it?

Although my husband and I seldom got to hockey games, we were nonetheless glued to the television set whenever our beloved team played. Often at times together and, sometimes, apart.

One night, when we were still 'courting', my future husband called to tell me that he was watching the game on

TV and that every time his team scored, he would eat a package of caramel snack cakes. There were two in a package, each of them delightfully oozing with caramel that seeped all over the white sponge cake, just beneath the luscious chocolate coating.

It wasn't long before the phone rang.

"They just scored. I'm eating the cakes now."

Two more calls came through to me during the first period. Two more in the second. And three additional ones after that.

In all, my future husband ate an entire box of the snack cakes that night. The last call was the most painful.

"I can't believe they scored again," he groaned. "I'm not sure I can eat another round but I said that I would, so I guess I will. Remind me not to do this ever again."

Regardless of that win, his team didn't make the playoffs that year. But still, he kept his hope alive.

"Next year. It's going to be next year that they win the Cup," he would say.

During that first 'meet-and-greet' dinner with my father and step-mother, it soon became apparent that my future husband could hold his own against my father's breadth of hockey knowledge. Finally, after yet another round of discussion where the two would argue the merits of some hockey player long-since retired, my father slammed his glass down in frustration.

"How the hell old are you?" he bellowed.

Although my husband was almost 11 years my senior, he certainly didn't look it. He remained young at heart—and physically—up until almost the day he died.

But this youthfulness could often prove problematic.

We were in Las Vegas one winter to attend the annual industry trade show. We were out for dinner at a swanky restaurant in Caesar's Palace with my husband's boss and his wife. My husband and I had been to FAO Swartz earlier that evening and had spotted a four-foot high, plush polar bear. (Polar bears were a bit of a hobby with us. It started out as a sort of gag and slowly became a living, breathing thing of its own. More on this later.)

The price tag at FAO Swartz was US$3,000. And although the bear was certainly a good one in terms of its resemblance to a real polar bear, it was an extravagance that we could ill afford.

The dinner went well, as did the wine that complemented it. It wasn't long before my husband let the news out of the bag.

"So, we were at FAO Schwartz earlier and we spotted a polar bear," he revealed. "It is a great replica, one that I think we should buy. But my wife doesn't agree with me. What do you two think?"

Up until then, our Vegas jaunts had resulted in much smaller purchases.

"If I win $100, then we should buy that polar bear sculpture for $175," my husband would say to me, as he continued to put coins into the slot machine. Part of me would hope for a big win that we could use to pay off the mortgage and start thinking of retirement, and part of me would hope against any kind of win to ward off the potential purchase of another polar bear knick-knack. Times were tough at this point and we often had problems meeting our bills at the end of the month.

"Why don't we wait and see. We can decide later," I would answer.

But inevitably, he would win just enough to 'convince' himself that it warranted a purchase of some sort. Needless to say, we always came away from Vegas with more bills than we could handle.

This night, my husband regaled his boss and his wife with enough information about the FAO Schwartz polar bear to get all of us to tromp over to the store to see it in the 'flesh'. By this point, I had indulged in my share of alcohol and was feeling my regular 'ole feisty self. When the conversation got to the point of no return, I knew we were done for and so, I began the bartering process in earnest.

The next morning, with a fuzzy memory and a full-on headache to boot, I turned to my husband.

"Tell me that we did not buy that polar bear last night," I pleaded.

"Oh no, but you did," he replied, a huge grin on his face. "And you drove a hard bargain. All in, including shipping and taxes, it came to only US$3,000."

I groaned, rolled over and tried to bury my head under the pillow.

My husband, on the other hand, was pleased as punch for the rest of the trip.

When the polar bear finally arrived at the airport, my husband and a co-worker had to rent a van to pick it up. But the bear was so large that it didn't fit.

The two co-conspirators apparently broke into bouts of laughter right there and then on the tarmac. The airport workers had to de-crate the bear to get him into the vehicle.

But, I have to admit, he did look quite good once we got him home.

Chapter Four

It's proving very difficult for me to get my head around the fact that my husband has died. I knew that it was going to happen eventually. The oncologist and specialists were straightforward with us from the start.

"Unfortunately, the news isn't good," our oncologist says grimly, one day toward the end. "It seems like the latest round of drugs isn't having any effect on your numbers. The counts are way up."

After a bit of discussion, we discover that the oncologist actually pulled the short straw.

"No one here wanted to be the bearer of bad news," he confesses. "We didn't want to let you down."

My husband has become quite popular with the various staff at the numerous hospitals that have since become part of our routine. Always quick to use satire or wit, he remains very much the funny and affable individual I married all those years ago. As a result, these doctor consultations are more like personal visits. I know that the staff has become enamoured of him. And I am sorry that they feel so bad in giving us the news.

"That's okay," I reply, trying to alleviate the tension in the room. "Let's hope the next round will work."

But we all know that there are very few next rounds in our future.

Still, when the time finally does come, it catches us both by surprise. My husband has rebounded so many times over these past couple of years that the expectation for him to do so again has become ingrained in the two of us.

"I'm sure it's nothing serious," I say that night, as he groans in bed from the pain in his stomach.

"Can you get me another painkiller?" he gasps. "I think the dinner is causing some major indigestion."

Unfortunately, it's not indigestion that is wracking his frail body.

The memories of that night continue to haunt me. What we thought was yet another 'typical' bump in the road proved to be the most catastrophic of them all.

Is there something I should have done differently? Is it my fault for not insisting on going to the hospital right away? Would he have lived to see another day if I had? Was there a mistake made at the hospital? Had I missed it?

As I try to cope with this new reality, I can't help but feel that there was something I missed doing in the old one. For some reason, my mind can't shut off. I feel guilty. Surely, there was something I could have done.

I remember how, early in the treatment process, I forgot to administer his chemotherapy pills. In fact, I missed giving the drug for a full eight days—too mixed up with appointments and schedules to get it right. Once I realized my error, I was beside myself with worry. How could I have done that? How could I have been so irresponsible? What would happen now?

It was days later before I could summon up the courage to admit the lapse to my husband. And it was with great trepidation that I broke down and spoke of it to the oncologist.

"These things happen," he said. "Don't beat yourself up about it. What's done is done. But try to be more diligent in the future. You need to get this right."

Had this somehow contributed to my husband's demise? The incident happened very early on but still, could my negligence have been a cause in my husband's death?

The questions continue to arise, unbidden, but ever-present nonetheless.

Day in and day out, my mind continues to sift through the recent past, trying to pinpoint what went wrong. And trying to find a way for me to get through this nightmare without losing my mind.

The memories help. But they also make it worse, highlighting everything I've lost.

I sit at the table or on the couch in the safety of our house. There's the stained-glass polar bear window that we had commissioned for us. There's the polar bear soapstone sculpture that we bought in Quebec City (at an astronomical price no less!). The polar bear plate settings we got as Christmas gifts one year. The polar bear wine glasses from Edmonton. The polar bear beer glasses from Santa Fe. The list goes on. And the memories keep flooding back.

There is also the Chinese lucky cat 'toy' that my husband brought back from one of his business trips to Asia.

"This is the lucky cat that is said to bring money," he informed me, upon his return. "Every time his tail wags, it means money will soon follow."

Apparently, there was a huge variety of lucky cats from which to choose.

Our money cat is small in stature, about four inches high. He is made of plastic and bears a sweet, innocent smile on his face. The small solar panel ensures that his head and tail continue to sway for hours at a time.

Eventually, I will deplete our polar bear collection of many items, gently caressing them as I bundle them up for other destinations and other people. But this lucky money cat is one of the few things I hold onto. It's probably one of our least expensive items and it's become yellow with age.

But it serves as a constant reminder that maybe, just maybe, my husband should have opted for the lucky cat that promised longevity and good health.

Chapter Five

It's been a few weeks since my husband has died. I am slowly getting to the point where I can leave the house, our sanctuary. I've been out for coffee with my mother a couple of times. Have even gone for a run with my sister, which ended in me collapsing in a bawling heap on the sidewalk. But I had tried. And my sister said that this, in itself, was an accomplishment.

Today, I am going to see a fortune teller. I have had an extremely hard time of it these last few days and I honestly don't know what to do. I feel like I have had the very heart of me ripped out and stabbed a million times over. My body physically aches with my husband's absence.

And every time I open the kitchen cupboard, I see the array of different-coloured pills that line the shelves. I've been hoarding them for months now. Not sure how I would feel once this finally happened. And every morning, they seem to call out for my attention.

"Do it," they say. "You'll be together if you do."

But where is my husband? If I knew for sure that there was some place where he went and that I could join him wherever that was, I would down the pills in an instant. But that little bit of doubt keeps nagging at me and I can't decide.

"When you die, you need to send me a sign that you're okay," I said to my husband during the final weeks of his life. "You need to let me know somehow."

We have a flagpole in the backyard. A stupid idea because it had been placed too close to the pear tree so the flag inevitably ended up getting caught in the branches. It would be stuck there, high in the tree, for days at a time until one of us (usually me) went through the tedious process of removing the flagpole (we couldn't lower it because it had broken soon after we put it up) and freeing the flag before erecting the flagpole once again. And then, within days, it would get tangled up yet again.

"Why don't you untangle the flag from the tree?" I suggest to my husband one night. "That way, I will know it's a sign from you."

"Oh, that's small fry," he replies, with a gleam in his eye. "I can do better than that."

And so it was left.

I thought about that exchange as I drove to the fortune teller. The flag was stuck once again. No surprise there. And every morning I looked out to see if things had changed.

Nothing yet.

"You've come looking for answers," intones the fortune teller, when I finally settle myself down in front of her large, wooden desk. "You're seeking something from me."

I had visited her before on a couple of occasions. The first time she had said that I would be extremely happy in my marriage. The second, a few years ago, she had said that I would be very lonely. I had written her off at that point, thinking she was alluding to a divorce when I knew for a fact that my marriage was strong. But now, in desperation, I had come crawling back.

"You've just lost someone," she says. "And you've come to me because you're looking for him."

The tears let loose at this point and don't stop. She goes on to describe my husband—from his favourite foods to his unique laugh. All of it is spot on. I am like a man dying of thirst, drinking up everything she says and trying to make my husband real again. I lose myself in her words. But then she catches my attention with what she says next.

"You've been thinking of joining him."

Guilty. I am caught.

"It won't work," she continues. "You're not going to die. You will end up in a hospital in a vegetative state."

I don't know if she can actually 'visualize' this or whether she is just putting two and two together and trying to scare me. But I continue to listen intently.

"You have a sister who is very concerned about you," she persists. "And you have a cat that needs you."

My husband and I had taken in a stray years ago, which had promptly given birth to seven very ill and malnourished kittens. We had to bottle feed one in particular because it was so sick. I had taken the day shift and my husband the night. And the little kitten had grown to become the apple of my husband's eye. The two were inseparable. Until his death. She now clung to my side.

Minutes later, I am on my way home. Despite having gone through almost the entire box of tissues on her desk, I continue to weep during the hour-long trip back. As I pull into the driveway, I see my father's SUV. I know he doesn't have a key to the house so I wander out back to determine where he is. And there, just as I round the corner into the backyard, I see him untangling the flag from the tree.

It feels like my heart has stopped. How can my husband free the flag and let me know he is okay if my father is doing it instead?

"What are you doing?" I scream, stomping over to try to put an end to it.

"This has bothered me for a few days now," my father calmly replies. I'm sure he notices my swollen red eyes and wonders where I have been. But being who he is, he doesn't say a word. "I'm just going to fix this for you and then I will be on my way."

That's my father. Don't talk about the obvious. If there is an emotion of any sort lurking about, the best tact is always ignorance. Don't acknowledge it and it will eventually go away. An interesting philosophy but not necessarily one of life's best practices. Still, it works for him. Sort of.

"That's nice of you," I reply, feeling a wave of exhaustion come over me yet again. "Thanks."

I turn away, eager for the comfort of my sanctuary. Life outside is proving too stressful.

Chapter Six

The nights are the worst. And the days. And all of the times in between.

I think of my husband every waking minute. I cry constantly. In fact, there is a small part of me that is amazed at the volume of tears I can shed and at how many times I can shed them in a day. The human body does have its wonders.

But right now, there is little wonder in my life. My body is going through the motions. I force myself to eat when I am not hungry. I crave glass after glass of wine. And then I sleep like I have never slept before.

And each night brings a different adventure with my husband. We re-live past episodes or we encounter new ones. But it is always the two of us. And we're so damn happy that it breaks my heart anew each time I awake and realize it will never be again.

I see elderly people walking down the street, hand in hand. Their lives forever intertwined, having lived life to the fullest and now enjoying the quiet comfort of friendship that only many years of marriage can bring.

And I want to run out and yell at them, "Why not you? Why did it have to happen to us? Why couldn't we get old together?"

But no one ever answers. And the questions reverberate over and over again in my head. I go through all of the marriages I know. Some are horrid, doomed to fail in a few years' time. Some are fraught with despair, an alcoholic here, a philanderer there.

"Why not them?" I scream internally so no one can know just how selfish I have become. "Why not them?"

Today is my first real outing. I am going to the Cottage Show with my sister. I don't own a cottage and have never wanted one.

"It will be fun," my sister insists, when trying to coax me out. "It will be good for you."

It's hours later and we're at the show. My sister and her husband are pretending that everything is fine but I know that they are watching my every move.

"Do you want something to eat? Do you need to sit down? How are you feeling?"

They're trying. I know they are. But really, my heart just isn't into this.

I turn into another seemingly endless aisle, feigning interest.

"Hey, imagine running into you here? How are you? It's been so long since we've seen each other? What's new?"

It's an old colleague of mine, one who moved onto greener pastures years ago.

"How's your husband?" she asks. "Is he here?"

Like a deer caught in the headlights, I freeze. I can't move. I can't think. I can't do this.

"No, he couldn't make it today. I'm here with my sister and her husband." I squeak the words out of my parched mouth and hope that my feeling of helplessness isn't as apparent to her as it is to me. "In fact, I have to go and find them. We were supposed to meet up a few minutes ago."

I hightail it away from her as fast as I can and make my way to the parking lot, away from everyone's prying eyes. I call my sister on her cell phone and tell her I am heading home.

Years ago, my husband surprised me with a birthday gift of a polar bear knapsack filled to the brim with mini tootsie rolls. I am very fond of them. He and I would watch movies for hours at a time, eating these tootsie rolls one after the other. It wasn't too long before the little knapsack was empty. We hung it on the door handle of our living room, the one leading into the kitchen.

I glance at it almost every day, a fond reminder of a special occasion.

When I walk into the house, I am immediately met with a sense that something has changed. I have been spending all my waking—and sleeping—hours within these four walls and am intimately familiar with every nuance.

First off, I check to see if the cat is okay. She is. And then I carefully look around. And see it.

The polar bear knapsack has moved from the living-room door handle to the one on the outside patio door. I look again, doubting what my eyes are showing me. But it has moved. I definitely left it on the handle of the living-room door leading into the kitchen. In fact, it had been there for years. And now it is on the handle of the patio door—the one facing the flag that has once again become entangled in the tree.

Is this the sign that my husband promised to send me? If so, what does it mean?

Chapter Seven

Shortly after my husband's diagnosis, we opted to bite the bullet and book a two-week Mediterranean cruise. We travelled a fair bit during our marriage, for business and pleasure. We had taken smaller river cruises in the past, enjoying the more intimate atmosphere provided. But had never been on a large cruise ship. Both my sister and mother cruised regularly and spoke highly of the experience.

My husband and I went all out and booked one of the two penthouse suites available. It was a glorious suite with blonde oak paneling, a private balcony, a sitting room and a fair-sized bathroom. There was even a walk-in closet.

Every morning, we would follow the crowds to the breakfast buffet. Throughout his treatment, my husband never lost his appetite. And the cruise was no exception. We would mosey up to the table, filling our plates with French toast, eggs, pancakes and all other sorts of enticing dishes.

After breakfast, we would retire to our suite for a brief rest before emerging again to stand in line for the appropriate tour of the day. Each one was as wondrous as the one before. We visited medieval churches, castles, towns and ancient sites— all of which were steeped in history. There were cafés, restaurants and sweet shops scattered throughout, interspersed with a bit of walking and plenty of photography. My husband was an avid photographer.

Unfortunately, my husband and I became separated on one of these tours. We were alone at the time, away from the rest of the tour group. We hadn't thought to bring cell phones so there was no way to get in touch with the other. The slow panic I felt initially quickly grew in intensity until I was almost running through the streets trying to find him. Had he fallen? Collapsed? Hurt himself? Where could he have gone?

Honestly, it was just one quick glance and maybe a short stroll down an alley and suddenly he was gone. I was beside myself with worry. Would we need a hospital? Would we miss the ship? How would we get home?

Eventually, I did find him. He was calmly sitting down at the sea, taking photographs of the pleasure craft that were bobbing about. He hadn't even noticed that I was gone.

In all, we were separated for about 20 minutes. It was the longest 20 minutes of my life. At the time, I wondered if this was what it would feel like when he was gone. If I would awake in a panic, unsure of where he had disappeared to or why he wasn't answering me. Was this a precursor of things to come?

The days' tours always ended at a meeting point, from which we would be transported back to the ship. We'd have time to relax onboard for a couple of hours—maybe take in a piano recital in the ship's atrium—before heading out for dinner.

But always, without fail, there would come a knock on the door, announcing the arrival of the day's delicacy. Chocolate-covered strawberries. Chocolate profiteroles. Assorted candies. Biscuits. Every evening at around 6:15, the knock would come. And the treat would appear.

At first, my husband and I were overwhelmed with the gesture. Surely this couldn't happen every single night. We couldn't be expected to eat all of these. But try we did. And by the end of the first week, we were eagerly awaiting that subtle knock and gleefully swinging open the door.

It wasn't long before my husband was unable to bend down to tie up his shoes. We would collapse in laughter as I took over the task, helping him dress for the late-night dinner that awaited.

Dinner onboard was a formal, sit-down affair. It was also one of the hardest times of the day for me. There would inevitably be talk of where you are from, why you are here and what your life story was. I was always on my guard, resisting all attempts to get too close to our story. Ours was a private one, not for general consumption. My husband, on the other hand, was more open about his experience. It became a constant juggle on my part to offset some of his more revealing remarks with ambiguity—to try to get them off the scent.

After a nightcap, my husband and I would more often than not retire to our room. There, we would pore over the day's photos—each one already a reminder of time past.

It is this collection of photos that I spend hours upon hours gazing at, now in the sanctuary of my home, wishing that I had stood behind the camera more often in order to freeze my husband in these special moments in time. Watching photo after photo as each scrolls across my computer screen provides solace to my soul. It's a happy remembrance of good times but a sad reminder of all that has been lost.

"There will come a time when you will be able to think of your husband without crying, when you will be able to think of him and be happy for the time that you've had together," my sister says to me one day, after another inevitable bout of tears. "I promise you, that day will come."

Chapter Eight

Things aren't getting any better. They remain as bleak as the day my husband died. Each hour rolls into the next. And I don't feel any differently. In fact, I don't think I am feeling anything at all.

After weeks and months of going for treatments, rushing to emergency rooms and seeing specialist after specialist, this surplus of inactivity seems especially overwhelming. I can't summon the energy that I had before. I don't have appointments to arrange. No drugs to order. I have too much time on my hands.

It used to be that I juggled work with scheduling appointments, counting out the proper pills for each day, taking note of symptoms or adverse reactions, and contacting specialists when my husband was feeling particularly bad.

When he was first diagnosed, we booked an appointment with a naturopath. I can't remember how it came to be. Someone must have suggested it and we probably thought it was a good idea at the time.

When we meet with the practitioner and settle ourselves in her office, the first thing she questions my husband about is his nationality. He reports that his mother is Austrian-German and his father Hungarian.

"Oh, that explains it," she states. I sit there wondering how 'that' explains anything. "Your European background puts you at a disadvantage. It is because of this that your body is prone to the disease."

At this point, I think she is a quack. But I want to be supportive of my husband (who often tells me that I am quick to rush to judgement) so I remain mute and feign interest.

"Of course, you will have to change your entire way of eating," she continues.

I know that my husband is fond of food. He isn't a foodie by any stretch. But he likes his bread, cheese and pâté. And he loves dessert, any kind and any flavour.

"You will have to eliminate all processed foods. And you will have to go on a gluten-free diet," she informs us. "This disease loves sugar. You have to stop feeding it."

I don't remember her being a specialist in this particular field of medicine but for the sake of argument, I remain silent.

"And you," she continues, looking over at me, "you will have to put your life on hold so that you can focus solely on your husband."

I am a bit taken aback and query, "What about my job? I still need to make money."

In fact, we needed to make a lot of money.

One of the drugs used in my husband's treatment was thalidomide, the same medication that resulted in catastrophic consequences in the early 1960s when many doctors prescribed it to pregnant women as a way to combat morning sickness.

"It is a very expensive drug," our oncologist tells us, as he writes the prescription. "But don't worry. The drug company that manufactures it has what's called a 'patient-assistance program', which will enable you to get access to the drug for free. In all the years I have been prescribing it, I have never had a case where the patient didn't qualify."

He hands us a sheaf of paperwork.

Later that week, while filling out the forms at home, I wonder just how 'truthful' we should be about our income. The forms ask for detailed financial data on the two of us and although the manufacturer doesn't say it will double-check with Canada Revenue Agency, it does caution against dishonesty.

In for a penny, in for a pound. I truthfully report our numbers.

It is weeks later that the oncologist calls to tell us that we have been denied access to the program and that we will have to foot the entire bill ourselves. The first time this has happened in his career—apparently.

"I'm truly sorry," he says. "I can't believe they turned you down."

Okay, it isn't that we are rich. I mean we struggle each month to pay our bills. But maybe we are living too much of the high life. I don't know. I can't imagine that we are the only ones with this dreadful disease who make a half-decent income.

"The cheapest place to get the drug is from England," advises the oncologist. "You can order two months' worth at a time. It works out to around $3,000 Canadian."

And now the naturopath is telling me that I have to put my work on hold and focus on my husband and his health. How can I do that, while still managing to pay our bills?

Turns out that I needn't have worried.

A huge shopping spree at the local health store and about three weeks under the new regime were all it took.

"I know I'm dying," my husband says to me one night, after another tasteless meal that I had lovingly prepared from all the 'right' foods. "But I would rather be happy and die sooner than continue eating this stuff. It's truly awful."

I gleefully throw out all the 'healthy' foodstuffs the next day.

We are back in business.

Chapter Nine

Shortly before my husband died, my mother, sister and I booked a trip to Las Vegas. A much-needed little jaunt to get away for a few days. I asked my husband's sister to come over and stay with him while we were away.

She had married at a very young age and had been travelling with her husband during the years since. Every three years, they would move to a different locale so it wasn't often that she and my husband were able to spend time together. She jumped at the opportunity to spend some quality time with her brother.

The arrangements worked out perfectly for everyone. The plane tickets were booked and the hotel room ordered.

But time was against us on this round. My husband died three weeks before our departure date.

I desperately wanted to cancel the trip but both my mother and sister urged me to leave it be.

"You're still in shock. You don't know whether you're coming or going at this point. Why don't you wait and see how you feel?" they counselled. "It could be just what you need."

What I needed, I thought to myself, was to be in my house alone; a place where I could still live and breathe the life that my husband and I had so carefully created. I craved closeness to our things, to what used to be us.

Inevitably, the day comes when we have to decide one way or the other. After much cajoling, I opt to go ahead.

The morning of the flight, I remember being terrified at the thought of leaving the house. Would the pets be okay? Would the house be alright? Is my husband still here, at least in spirit? Will he wonder where I am?

During the plane ride itself, I am stricken with an intense fear of flying. The slightest bit of turbulence sends my heart racing. I begin gasping for air.

I had been fine whenever I flew with my husband, calm in the belief that if the plane were to plummet to the earth, then we would be facing it together. Whatever was to be, was to be.

This safety net of mine seems to have vanished with the loss of my husband. There is no more 'we'. It is now 'me, myself and I'. And I don't like it one teeny-weeny bit.

The four days in Vegas go by in a blur. I spend most of them sleeping, off in my dreams with my now late husband. My mother and sister tiptoe around me, letting me sleep for the most part and, occasionally, trying to entice me with walks and dinners. I can barely eat and long again for the safety of my house.

"Try to eat something," my mother says, as I gingerly lift yet another tablespoon of soup to my mouth. "Your body needs nourishment."

But despite my best efforts, I can't even stomach the thought of food. The smell alone makes me nauseous.

"I'll just have a glass of wine," I weakly reply. And blessedly, my mother doesn't say a word.

As we are leaving the hotel room one morning for yet another of those painfully long luncheons, we pass by a string of slot machines in the lobby.

My husband and I would always play the slots whenever we were in Vegas. He would often be at one press conference and I at another. So we would usually arrange to meet at a certain hotel in front of a particular bank of machines.

One of the more popular games at the time featured three frogs and a prince. We played it often. But we never won any significant amount. Just enough, typically, for my husband to convince himself (and me) that the winnings merited another polar bear purchase of some sort.

Although my mother, sister and I pass the same slot machines many times over the course of a day, I fail to notice this particular game. Until one afternoon when we are returning after another endless walk.

I tell my mother and sister that this is fate. This had been one of our favourite games. How could I have missed it? I have to play at least US$20. I have to do it for my husband and me. For old times' sake.

Fortunately, it isn't too long before the little frogs are popping into princes all over the screen. I win US$1,000 within half an hour—the most my husband or I had ever won in Vegas.

Surely this is a sign from him that he is still by my side, watching over me. He hasn't left or, if he has, he hasn't really gone too far.

We are together again, in a way. Life is almost palatable.

Chapter Ten

My husband and I are having dinner at one of our favourite restaurants. We're making a list of what we want to buy. A wish list of sorts. He's got items like new consumer electronics equipment—a $10,000 receiver—and I have things like a new couch and a trip to Europe. We're both having a wonderful time and are happily giggling over the potential.

Two days before, we had sold a piece of property. And surprisingly to us, we actually made a bit of money.

Throughout our marriage, I had long searched for that perfect piece of land in the middle of nowhere on which my husband and I could build our own custom house. My father was already on his fourth such residence and I desperately wanted to follow suit.

Although my husband and I both loved the place that we had, we were only too aware of the encroachment of civilization. It wouldn't be long before we ended up in the middle of suburbia. And neither of us wanted that.

My father and I (my husband joined us initially but soon tired of it) would often drive through the local countryside, aimlessly going up and down the back roads in search of the latest gem of a real-estate bargain.

On occasion, we would stumble across something that looked promising, only to have our hopes dashed for one reason or another.

This time around, we actually found a parcel of land that seemed suitable and, after much persuasion, my husband finally gave in and agreed to make the down payment.

Within a few weeks, it was ours.

"I think we'll call it 'Blossom Hill'," I say to my dad, as we trudge up the steep slope that characterizes the four-acre property peppered with a myriad of apple trees. "I want to build right here on the top of the hill."

"It will make for a long driveway, a tough one to manoeuver in the winter," he replies. "But it could work. Let me make a few calls and see what we can do."

My father had assumed the role of general contractor on all of his past houses. It was a task he thoroughly enjoyed and one that I hoped to reap the benefits of in the near future.

But Blossom Hill was not to be. The terrain proved too difficult to overcome and the cost too high to build. Plus, as my husband was wont to remind me, it would add another 30 minutes to his daily commute. Not a prospect he looked forward to.

So we put Blossom Hill up for sale. And we waited. And waited. And waited. Eventually, we received an offer, one that netted us a cool $50,000.

And that's why we are currently sitting in the restaurant, feverishly making a list.

"If I say yes to your receiver, will you agree to the new couch and a trip to Europe?" I venture. "And we also have to hold some money back for a down payment for the next piece of property we buy."

My husband's groan shows his response to the idea of buying yet more land. But the list proves too tantalizing.

"If I say yes to the above, can I also get a new TV?" he banters back.

"No. I don't think we can add a TV into the mix. At least, not yet. Let's move it over to the 'possible' category," I reply.

Eventually, we do agree on a list of purchases. The receiver is in. The couch is out. And the trip to Europe is on.

Better yet, my father and I can continue our search because we have the down payment in the bank.

And, amazingly, it is my husband who finally discovers the perfect property.

"I think I found it," he says to me one day. "It's south of where we are now so my commute will be less. And it's eight acres of beautiful trees. Not a soul in sight. I think this is the one."

A quick call to my father and a visit thereafter proves him correct. We do the deal and, within days, the property is ours.

"I'm sitting in my truck on your new property right now and do you know what I see?" my father asks me, after I answer the phone one morning.

"No idea," I reply, immediately thinking that there is some flaw with the property that will make it unsuitable for us to build. Will we have to start the search all over again? "Is there a problem?"

"No problem," he replies. "In fact, quite the opposite. There are six deer just off to the right of me. They've been here for about five minutes now and don't look like they are in any rush to leave. I think your property is part of their territory."

I am thrilled. Both my husband and I are huge animal lovers.

One night, on a desolate country lane, we had come across a rabbit that had been hit by a car. It was lying in shock in the middle of the road. I tried to rescue it while my husband used his cell phone to call the 24-hour emergency veterinary service. We sped off in the dark to the clinic, where the veterinarian told us he would have to put the rabbit down, that one of its hind legs had been shattered and it would never survive in the wild.

With my jeans bloodied from holding the poor thing on my lap during the ride, I tentatively asked the vet if we could pay for the surgery and build the rabbit an enclosure on our property. My husband eagerly agreed and chimed in as well.

"I just don't think it would be fair to the rabbit," said the vet. "It wouldn't be a real life. I can't sanction you two doing that."

My husband and I were devastated that night. I cried for days afterwards.

With deer on our new property, however, we will be able to sit by the window with our morning cups of coffee and see the wildlife go about their daily routine. Does life get any better than that?

A few visits to the architect and we have the perfect dream house ready to go on the perfect dream property. Everything is falling into place. Life is good.

And then a few weeks later, we get the diagnosis.

The land is one of the first things that we have to let go. We can't fight this disease on one front while orchestrating a new build and a move on another.

"We can wait and see what will happen," my husband says to me, knowing how much this dream means to me. "We can put things on hold for a while."

But I am painfully aware of the fact that we aren't in a position financially to carry the debt for very long. And deep down inside, I know that the news is not good. As much as I hope and long for things to turn out alright, in my heart of hearts, I have a very bad feeling that things are about to turn for the worse.

And that they do.

Chapter Eleven

My husband and I both love to travel. Fortunately, our jobs allow us to do so without having to pay that much extra for the pleasure.

One of my first international business trips takes place while we are still dating. I am heading to Germany for a trade show. Although I am excited about the upcoming adventure, I am loathe to leave—even if it is only for a few days. We spend every waking moment together leading up to the trip.

But finally, the morning of departure arrives. Somewhat glum, we get in the car and head to the airport. Unknown to us, there has been a huge accident on the highway. We come to an abrupt stop shortly after we enter the major thoroughfare. Stuck with nowhere to go, along with hundreds of other cars.

Neither of us is worried initially, as we had accounted for a lot of extra time. But as the minutes tick by, we become increasingly anxious. I can't miss the flight, no matter what.

Finally, after sitting for about two hours without moving an inch, my 'boyfriend' opts to drive on the shoulder. We both know it is illegal and are terrified. But we feel we have little choice.

Doing speeds of up to 150 kilometres per hour (when finally able to do so!), he pulls up to the airport within minutes of my flight. He drops me off at the door, gives me a peck on the cheek and says that he will find a parking spot and try to come back to say farewell.

I rush inside and race up to the desk.

"Have I missed my flight?" I anxiously ask the attendant standing behind the counter. "There was a huge accident on the highway and we were stuck for hours."

"Actually, you're a bit early," he replies, after perusing my ticket and checking with the system. "Twenty-four hours to be exact. Your flight doesn't leave until this time tomorrow."

I am speechless. Seriously. We drove on the shoulder of a major highway and sped like the devil to get here and we are actually a day ahead. I can't believe it.

"My boyfriend is going to murder me," I utter. "We just about got killed on the way down here."

Right then, I see him race through the terminal's front doors. He is frantically looking in all directions.

"Is that him?" asks the airline representative.

"Yes," I reply.

The attendant quickly stands in front of me (I guess he had taken me at my word when, in actuality, I do tend to exaggerate in these types of situations).

"Sir, I have something to tell you. I need you to stay calm," he states.

My boyfriend looks just as bewildered as I feel. He stands still and waits.

"It turns out your girlfriend is a day early. Her flight doesn't leave until tomorrow. We can either book her on the next flight, which is leaving tonight, or we can send you home and you can come back tomorrow."

My future husband turns to me with a huge grin on his face.

"We will come back tomorrow," he replies. "We're happy to have the extra day together."

It's times like these that I knew I was smitten. Our marriage was meant to be.

Even after we were married, my husband and I kept up our love of travel. Although we struggled financially at first, we never turned down a potential travel opportunity. But, we definitely had to keep an eye on our money.

Whenever we could, we would take advantage of business trips to schedule a little extra vacation time for the two of us. The flights would already be paid for, as would most of the hotel bills. It seemed the perfect way to satisfy our desire to travel with our insufficient funds.

One such occasion arose shortly after we were married. My husband was invited on a trip to Hong Kong. As a contributing writer to his magazine, I conned my way in as well. It was one of our first major international trips together. We were both so excited.

The company hosting the event put us up at what we thought was the swankiest hotel in Hong Kong. Our room was huge, with one wall made entirely of glass overlooking the harbour. We could see houseboats and other vessels gently bobbing on the water. At night, the lights shone in a myriad of different designs.

Each day, my husband and I were whisked away to visit factories, corporate headquarters and boardrooms, stopping periodically for gourmet lunches at impressive venues. The nights brought new adventures, like visits to local landmarks, lavish dinners and nightclubs. It was a time of great indulgence for both of us. We were literally treated like royalty.

Prior to leaving for Hong Kong, my husband and I opted to extend our stay by a few days. What were the chances that we would ever be back? We searched high and low for a reasonably priced hotel and eventually, after much consternation, found one.

So, as the business portion of our trip comes to a close, we find ourselves in a cab heading not to the airport with the rest of the 'dignitaries' but on our own into the unknown.

It isn't long before the cab driver pulls up in front of a dreary and tired-looking hotel that has certainly seen better days. We glance at each other, shrug our shoulders and pay the fare. Whatever will be, will be. We are determined to see the 'real' Hong Kong while we can.

Turns out our entire hotel room is the size of the bathroom in our previous suite. The concrete walls are painted a drab grey. Dimmed lighting flickers throughout the halls. It is a tale of two cities.

When we eventually stumble into our washroom, we discover almost an exact replica of one that you would find on an airplane. Made of pre-formed plastic, the tiny cubicle seems to have been dropped there from on high. It offers little room to turn around, never mind shower.

We both break out into laughter. Our new 'home' for the next few days is certainly a step down from what we have just experienced. But at least this time around, it will be just the two of us. No need for polite business discussion.

And, despite our humble surroundings, we end up having a wonderful vacation, one that still affords the nicest of memories—even in these cruel times.

Hong Kong isn't the only business trip that we take advantage of in order to help offset the cost of our personal travel. There is a long list of places: Mount Tremblant—where my husband proudly walked through the village holding onto a stuffed toy polar bear that measured three feet high (the latest of our additions at the time!); Banff and Lake Louise—where we fell in love with a $10,000 original oil painting (which I finally convinced my husband to abstain from purchasing!); and a host of other exciting venues.

One of the last business trips of this sort is Anaheim. At this point, we know that my husband is dying. And it brings a sense of tragedy to the trip. We try to mimic our upbeat sense of adventure that we had finely honed by this point—each of us attempting to stand strong for the other. But a dark foreboding looms over the entire trip. Even a visit to Disneyland fails to produce the familiar sense of joy that we are accustomed to feeling.

Sure, we do the requisite tourist attractions. We go whale watching. We visit the museums and galleries. We eat at the trendy restaurants.

But things have changed. We are no longer the carefree, *carpe diem* people we once were. We are adjusting to our new reality, one slow and painful step at a time.

Chapter Twelve

The days of extended business trips are well behind me now. In fact, even the days of getting out of the house are still limited. We had big plans to build a new home, to travel more and to move gracefully into retirement and old age. But sadly, those plans have been violently torn away.

Today, I am safely ensconced back in my sanctuary. I let out a huge sigh of relief and take a look around me. In the end, I can honestly say that I am happy that my husband and I didn't get the chance to build our dream home. Not because it wasn't the right decision for us or one made in haste. No, it's because I now have 20 years of memories in which to surround myself day in and day out.

And it is these recollections that help keep me sane. Even the house itself is a product of our design, or rather my husband's father, who was an architect.

It isn't long after my husband proposes to me that plans for our sanctuary are soon underway. The proposal, by the way, amounts to my husband wordlessly slipping a ring on my finger one night while we are laying prone on the couch, watching the hockey game. I 'romantically' respond by asking, "What's this?"

My husband counters—just as romantically I should say, "What do you think it is? It's a ring."

And thus, just like in the fairy tales (or a close approximation thereof!), our fates are sealed.

The house itself is an old school house set in the middle of the countryside. Any errand means a minimum drive of either 20 minutes to the south or 20 minutes to the north. And even then, you are hard pressed to describe what you find there as anything more than the equivalent of a town.

At the time of our purchase, the school house had already been converted into a home. The original one-room design had been segmented into two bedrooms, a kitchen, living/dining room and a bathroom. A semi-finished concrete basement lurked underneath and a detached two-car garage was situated just to the north.

A couple of brief conversations and a few visits with my husband's father soon produce a set of modern drawings that essentially re-open the cramped spaces, creating a wonderfully light and airy interior that measures approximately 30 x 30 feet, complemented by ceilings that soar close to 12 feet high. The south wall incorporates the bank of windows inherent in the original school house design, opening the room to sunlight and prominently displaying the leaves of the huge 100-year-old maple tree that stands proudly nearby.

It often feels like we are living in a tree house.

The boys' and girls' cloakrooms are soon transformed into a modern, Ikea-style kitchen with a raised countertop, bar stools (which took us months to find, as my husband was all about comfort, while I was all about design), and all the modern-day appliances (minus the dishwasher, as neither of us cooked so there was no need for one).

The architectural design also incorporates the addition of a bedroom and ensuite bathroom, with a sound-proofed audio/video studio located underneath.

Situated on a one-acre parcel of land, there is plenty of privacy and greenery. We eventually add a lap pool and, years later, a hot tub.

It is an oasis all of our own making. And one perfectly suited to just the two of us. But then again, it was always about just the two of us.

Although, at times, others did intrude.

"I am going to call your mother," my husband threatens me one day. "I don't know what else to do."

It is three days before our wedding. We are to be married in our beloved little school house. For the last six months, my husband and I have lived in the midst of demolition and

47

renovation. It has been a life of horse hair and plaster—the fine particulates of either one or the other getting into everything we own, including our clothes.

In order to save money, we have taken on some of the demolition work ourselves. It is while we are removing studs from the living-room walls one day that the ceiling begins to sag. In horror, I watch as the next stud, once removed, causes a further dip.

"I'm getting out of here," I scream, running off to grab the cat and escape to the safety of the back lawn. "The whole ceiling is going to collapse."

My husband stands his ground, confident in the expertise of his father's design. He calmly instructs me to get back inside and to help him prop up the ceiling until he can get a hold of his father for further instruction.

It is a minor calamity but one that passes quickly. Just as is being awakened each morning, by a handful of workers ready to start the day at some ungodly hour, while we are sleeping in the middle of the construction zone on nothing but a mattress on the floor.

But we do manage to get through all of these hurdles without too much trouble (I can say that now!).

Nevertheless, this afternoon is the final straw that does me in—the stress of the demolition, renovation and wedding proving too much for me to bear. Our long-awaited carpet has failed to arrive. And, on top of that, it will need a minimum of two days to settle before it can be installed. Otherwise, stretching will occur and unsightly lumps will form.

It is this last telephone call informing me of the latest carpet delay that has sent me scurrying into bed. And there I stay for the next 24 hours, despite the constant cajoling and pleading of my soon-to-be husband.

"You have to get yourself out of bed," my mother admonishes me, after she has made the long trek north in answer to my future husband's cry for help. "Lying in bed isn't doing you any good. You're only creating more stress for yourself and everyone else."

She towers over me, refusing to budge. Every time I raise the covers to my face, she reaches out and brings them back down. And during it all, she natters and natters non-stop.

Eventually, my mother's 'sweet talk' works its magic. I finally get out of bed and surprisingly, everything that needs to get done before the wedding ceremony gets done. Even the carpet is laid. (Mind you, we did have to get it stretched and cut a couple months afterwards.)

The ceremony goes off without a hitch, although I am shaking so badly that the baby's breadth from my bouquet ends up strewn all around my feet.

Of course, I am wearing the traditional white wedding dress. Even though I had never intended to do so. And there is a large reception that night as well. Again, even though we hadn't wanted one.

"I'm holding a party in honour of your wedding and it would be nice if you two could be there," my father announces to us one day.

As soon as we acquiesce, the wedding dress comes next.

"No one will know who the bride is if you don't wear the traditional dress," declares my mother, in response to my announcement that I plan on wearing a simple cocktail dress.

"If they don't know who the bride is, then they shouldn't be at the wedding," I adamantly shoot back.

But, like most things when it comes to my mother, I lose the battle. In the end, what we had envisioned as a small and quiet 'drop-in' reception at the school house ends up involving some 100+ people at a grand reception in a rented hall.

I don't begrudge the event now. Looking back, I can even admit that it was fun.

It's hard to believe that it all happened more than 20 years ago. Seems like a long time and short time—both at the same time.

It is there, at the school house, that my husband and I would while away the hours, content in our solitude. We'd have special movie days when we would unplug the phone, rent a handful of movies (back when there were still video rental stores) and load up on junk food. We'd sit—transfixed—for hours at a time, taking bathroom breaks when necessary but otherwise undisturbed in our indulgence.

"I tried calling you all day on Saturday and there was no answer," my sister or mother would inevitably say to me the next day. "Where were you guys?"

I would try to explain—even invite one or both of them to join us for the next event—but they couldn't understand. To them, we lived alone and had no children so there was no need for what they perceived as yet another form of solitude. To us, they were happy times. We lived for those weekends when our schedules allowed us to partake in our viewing pleasure.

Being involved in the consumer electronics industry, my husband was one of the first to purchase a video laser disc player. Of course, the fact that we lived miles north of any major city that would have a glimmer of hope of stocking the discs didn't hold him back.

So, in addition to renting videos from the local retailer, the two of us would often venture down into the 'big smoke' to visit the one or two high-end, specialty retailers that sold the discs. The selection, at this time, was rather limited, but regardless, we always managed to find something that looked appealing. More often than not, it was the movie classics that we would gravitate towards, titles like *High Noon*, *The Producers* and *The Turn of the Screw*.

After dropping down several hundred dollars, we would make our way back home with our beloved 'treasures', content in the knowledge that there would be several more movie days in our future.

Chapter Thirteen

It's been about two months now since my husband died. I still wait for the sound of his car in the driveway every night, my mind convinced that he is on one of his many business trips and will be back any minute. In fact, there are actual moments when I think I hear his side of the garage door opening. I get up eagerly and run to the window, only to realize that it's my mind playing tricks on me. He won't be coming home any time soon.

I constantly think of him when small things happen during the day, automatically picking up the phone to call him at work. My eyes water when I go grocery shopping and see his favourite foods on the shelves. I even start crying when I see how a food supplier has added a new flavour to one of his grocery staples. How I would have loved to buy it and bring it home for him as a surprise. He would have been thrilled.

My days have become a series of what ifs and wants. I'm still living very much in the recent past. And it seems to be taking an awfully long time for this to sink in.

I continue to plod away at some semblance of reality. I am really just going through the motions. But I hold onto the hope that things will change for the better—eventually.

Today, I am selling my husband's beloved car. My dad made all of the arrangements. Thank God. I wouldn't have been able to handle doing it on my own.

"That's what fathers are for," he says, when I first ask him. I can't bear to see the sight of the car in our garage. My husband loved that car so much that it breaks my heart to see it there without him. And my heart needs to mend.

I am an emotional wreck of course. My husband and I had always taken his car whenever we went out together. He was like my own personal chauffeur. We would spend hours driving about the countryside or heading into the city for a dinner with friends. And it was always my husband who drove. He had owned a few different cars over the years but this one was, by far, the most cherished of them all. I sometimes wondered whether he loved that car more than me.

And today will be one of the first—and last—times that I drive it.

I head out of the driveway, with my father following in his SUV. I start to cry the minute I get into the car and continue crying all of the way to the dealer's. I can't even look the manager in the eye, just sit there and cry and sign wherever he points. The ride back with my father is more of the same.

"I guess I'll just drop you off at home," he finally says, breaking the half-hour of silence that has been interspersed with sobs and periodic nose blowing.

"Thanks Dad," I sniffle. And escape back into the house.

I immediately look for signs, as I am wont to do these days every time I go out. I check each room to see if anything has changed. Nothing I can determine.

I am like a ship lost at sea, without an anchor. As a freelance writer, I work from home. The job has slowed down considerably in the last few weeks (of which I am extremely thankful). There are times when I have to conduct interviews over the phone—appreciative of the fact that the days of actually sitting in front of someone to do the interview are long over. I can maintain a false front for a few minutes at a time, the person on the other end of the phone none the wiser to the fact that my husband has just died—that my life is in pieces.

My husband was an editor but he was a writer at heart. He was the smartest man I had ever met. In fact, I was intimidated by him at first. We worked for the same publishing company. There was some going-away or welcoming party at the time. Back then, the parties for those leaving had become too plentiful so the owners had conceived the bright idea of holding welcoming parties instead.

Talk circled around to relationships and one of my girlfriends asked me what I was looking for in a man. I spoke about my romantic dreams and probably embellished them a tad more than usual. I guess I came across as being reminiscent of a young schoolgirl waiting for her knight in shining armor.

My husband, who was listening at the time but wasn't yet even my date, never mind my husband, had in the previous year, put an end to a very bad marriage.

"You make it sound like some guy on a white horse will sweep in and carry you off into the sunset," he quipped. "I pity the man who marries you because he is going to have to bear the responsibility of being the one to destroy your naïve idea of marriage."

A mere three years later, we were married. And truth to tell, my husband was my white knight in shining armour. And my naïve idea of marriage has remained intact.

I spend the rest of the day—and many days thereafter—searching through all of my husband's belongings, confident in the knowledge that he has written me a letter or provided me with some guidance on how I should go forward without him. He was, after all, a man of many words. His vocabulary and intellect were far sharper than mine. And he had seemed so complacent in his ill health. He didn't rage. He didn't scream. He didn't let loose in anger at the injustice of it all. He took everything in stride, maintaining his sense of honour and humour throughout. Surely he had scribbled down, somewhere, his words of advice to me, of how I could get over this murky abyss to the other side.

Chapter Fourteen

I am at a client's office, sitting in a back office methodically going about my work, when I get the call. It is February 14, 2008. Valentine's Day.

"Hi. It's me. I'm with the doctor getting the results of the scope and he says it looks like it's something called multiple myeloma," my husband reports.

"Oh. What does that mean?" I ask, already feeling guilty that I hadn't accompanied him for the results. So sure was I that it was nothing to worry about. Low hemoglobin. That was the issue. So maybe he hadn't been eating enough red meat. Nothing that a few pills couldn't fix. Or so I had thought at the time.

"He's sending me to a specialist but he says that most people with the disease live long and full lives."

His was not to be.

"Unfortunately, your case is further complicated by a chromosomal disorder," the oncologist says at one of our later meetings. "This means that the prognosis isn't as good."

My husband was given three years to live. He survived three years and one month.

A flurry of activity follows the diagnosis. There are the tests, the drugs, the procedures to boost white blood cell production in preparation for the stem-cell transplant. Then there is the transplant itself and the weeks of recovery afterwards. Then it is the chemotherapy. The transfusions. The adverse reactions. The infections. The hospital stays. Everything seems to flow right into the next. It is an endless stream of doctors, hospitals and procedures.

And none of it seems to work, at least for very long.

"Unfortunately, it looks like the drugs are losing their efficacy," the oncologist repeatedly says. "We'll try another drug."

And then it is: "Unfortunately, we're running out of drugs. We'll have to use a cocktail of them together."

Eventually, the cocktails run out as well. Or my husband's ability to withstand the toxic effects of them runs out.

Which brings me back to why I am rifling through all of my husband's things, trying to find words of advice that will show me the path forward. Aside from managing to turn the entire house upside down, I have nothing. No wise words. No special endearment. Nothing. How could he let me down like this? He had had hours on his own while I ran errands or cleaned or cooked or worked. Surely, he could have penned some small missive that I could grasp onto. How hard would it have been? Really? How he could not think of me once he was gone?

I remember my sister telling me the story of an acquaintance of hers who had lost her husband to cancer. He was so much in love that he arranged to have a special piece of jewellery delivered to her on each anniversary of their marriage—even after his death.

I remember thinking of how nice that would be, to be acknowledged year after year in that special way. To know that your husband, wherever he was, was still thinking of you. To be able to celebrate that gift of marriage—even after the one partner had passed away. How I wished that would happen to me.

"Turns out, the lady actually started dreading the anniversaries," my sister continued at the time. "What began as a pleasant surprise, soon became painful reminders of everything she had lost. All she really wanted to do was to try to get on with her life but, instead, the gifts haunted her with things past. She began dreading them. Eventually, she put a stop to them. Just couldn't handle it."

That surely wouldn't have been my reaction, I thought to myself at the time. I would have loved to receive his annual gifts, his way of acknowledging our time together. In a way, then, our marriage would never end. Right?

I know that there won't be any gift waiting for me on our anniversary. That was just the type of guy that my husband was. But that's okay. I certainly am not expecting anything like that. And truth to tell, I am not even thinking of our anniversary. I am still just trying to get through the day, whatever day that happens to be.

But I am hopeful that my husband has written something for me; that he has tried to provide some words of inspiration. Even a couple of sentences will do. Just something that I can take to heart and cherish, to help lessen the pain of losing him.

So here I am, desperately searching through his belongings for some small message, some direction.

"I think it's a lot harder on those who are being left behind," one of the patients at the hospital says to me one day, when my husband leaves for the washroom.

We are sitting in a communal area, each station outfitted with a patient in the midst of a transfusion of some sort. Most patients have someone with them to help sort through the complicated procedure of getting the blood work completed, waiting for the results and then coordinating with the harried nurses on what needs to be done.

"Oh, I don't think so," I answer the frail lady sitting in her chair. Her hair has long since gone—the result of multiple chemo treatments. She wears a brown bandana in its stead, complemented by a beige dressing gown and sandals. She is probably in her 60s but, wan and weak, looks late 70s instead.

Her eyes glitter as she peers into mine. Tears well instantly after she first speaks to me but I will them away with fierce determination.

"I think we have the easier part of it when compared to what you have to go through," I continue. "I don't think I could be as strong or determined as you or my husband for that matter. You seem to take all of this prodding and procedure as par for the course. So calm. I'm sure I'd be ranting and raving instead."

She smiles at me then, confident in the knowledge that I am a torrent of emotions on the inside with only a thin veneer to protect me. She makes eye contact once again, seems to nod ever so slightly and then puts her head down to concentrate on her knitting.

Not having the courage to carry on the conversation, I glance anxiously at my watch instead and wait for my husband's return. It is going to be another long struggle through the afternoon commute in order to get back home. And we haven't even been to the pharmacy yet to get this week's assortment of drugs. That, in itself, will probably take another hour. Which means we will be heading back at the same time as every other person in the city. It will be dark before we get home.

As much as I have come to expect these long days of driving and waiting and driving, I still have a hard time being patient. It is as though I have to travel at a constant 120 kilometres per hour to remain in front of this encroaching disease that is rushing after us at an unbreakable speed. I need to stay ahead, to be in control. And to make sure that everything that can be done is being done.

I am invincible—on the outside at least.

I often spend the time in these communal hospital areas watching other couples to see if I can uncover some secret on how they cope. I watch behind the cover of a magazine or a book, trying to listen to conversations. Sometimes, I actually engage them in discussion, attempting to determine what disease these people have, what the prognosis is, and what they are doing about it. I am so sure that there are answers out there but that I just haven't found them yet. If I keep looking hard enough, I will find them.

There is one lady in particular who is strikingly beautiful. Long red hair cascades over her shoulders. A lovely, engaging smile. And a lean but curvaceous body that screams femininity. I am envious of her in that way that all women are when they are self-conscious about their own body's inadequacies. And yet, she is the one who is dying. Her husband is a loving, attentive guy from what I can see. The two seem inseparable. I guess, in a way, I equate them to my husband and me. Obviously not the same in the looks department but definitely the same circumstances. We see them often during our numerous hospital appointments and I regularly compliment her on her hair.

It isn't until months later, as we are making one of those arduous and onerous treks out of the city towards home, that my husband informs me she wears a wig. I break down in tears.

Chapter Fifteen

We were lucky—my husband and I. In a certain way, I guess you could say. The disease never truly got him down until very close to the end. Sure, there were a couple 'bumps' along the road. Like the time we were scheduled to head to Miami with my mother and sister.

It was going to be a 'needed break'. Some place warm and inviting. A chance to go for a walk and lay on the beach. Just relax and try to escape the reality of the disease, at least for a few days.

We end up in the emergency room the night before our departure. My husband has developed a fever and we agree to proceed on the side of caution before the trip.

"Do you have a cat?" asks the emergency-room doctor. This is hours after awaiting the results of blood tests and CAT scans.

"Yes, we have three," I pipe up. By this point, my husband is exhausted and is trying to doze periodically between the constant barrage of pokes and prods.

"Well, your husband has an infection, more than likely from the saliva of one of your cats. It wouldn't be an issue for most people but given his weakened state, his body hasn't been able to fight it off. I am going to have to admit him. And I have already called for the specialist of infectious diseases."

This sounds rather ominous. A specialist in infectious diseases. I mean, we have three cats but they are your average domestic cats. They have had their shots. And they are all healthy.

Really, an infectious disease specialist.

"We're booked to be on a flight to Miami tomorrow," I venture, knowing the response that is coming but hopeful nonetheless. "Will we be able to make it? We're not leaving until one in the afternoon."

"I'm afraid not," comes the reply. "You won't be going anywhere."

I make the calls to my mother and sister and urge them to proceed without us.

"I think we should all cancel," says my sister, always on my side. "It won't be the same without you two."

I do feel for her, having to deal with our mother on her own for five days straight. I wouldn't wish that on anyone, never mind my best friend. But it will be good for her to get away. She has been a rock by my side for the past couple of years, more so as the disease progressed.

"Go. Have a good time. Just keep in touch, so we know what we're missing," I joke. "We will live vicariously through you."

Turns out that the infectious disease specialist keeps my husband in the hospital for a week. In isolation, no less. And that isn't the end of it. He continues to receive intravenous treatment for six weeks after his release. At least, he is able to be at home for that part of the treatment.

I couldn't help but look at our pets differently after that night. We had the three cats and an African Grey parrot. Every time I glanced their way, I would wonder about what other types of infectious bacteria they might be harbouring.

Luckily, we never ran into another pet-related episode. But the once proved more than enough.

From that night on, we are on high alert against germs. Essentially, we become big-time 'germophobes'. I begin doubling up on my vitamins. It wouldn't do to have me come down with something; even the common cold could end up putting my husband in the hospital.

We also begin getting the annual flu shot—a practice I continue to this day.

That Christmas, we discuss our options and decide to skip the family get-together. When we were first married, we would alternate Christmas at his parents one year and at mine the next. It was always a huge deal, with plenty of food, drinks and good fun.

Both his mother and father have since passed away so we have been spending the last couple of years with my parents (in fact, it is Christmas Eve at my father's and Christmas Day at my sister's—which is where we get to spend time with my mother).

By now, however, my sister and her husband have six children—all of whom have germ-carrying potential. With more chemo scheduled for early January, we opt to stay home and spend a quiet Christmas on our own. This would prove to be the first and last time we do so.

Neither of us being much of a cook, we arrange for a quiet night of nibbles and wine. A celebration of sorts but without the usual fanfare.

That afternoon, as we are settling down for the evening, our doorbell rings. Turns out that my sister and her husband had spent the entire morning making us a full-on Christmas dinner—complete with cranberries, turkey, stuffing and even dessert. They don't stay to chat. Just ring the bell, walk into the kitchen, give a brief explanation of what is what and then carry on their way.

Have I mentioned how my sister is my best friend? She is the only one I was able to stay in contact with during those first few weeks after the initial diagnosis. I cut off communication with everyone else, even my parents. Couldn't deal with their questions and concerns when I was so busy struggling to cope with my own new reality.

"Just send me an email, to let me know you're alright," my sister emails, after days without receiving any word from me. "You don't have to write anything. Just put 'Okay' in the subject line."

Every once in a while—whenever I can muster up the strength—I send her back a short reply. Even though there are very few of her emails that I do answer, I spend hours reading through her many paragraphs of commentary over and over again. More often than not, they contain mundane information about her job, her kids, our parents, the weather—whatever.

But for me, it is a connection back to the reality I once knew. It is a thin string that I can pull on any time I want or need.

As the weeks pass, I am able to write more in my emails to her. Eventually, I can even talk to her on the phone. But there were a lot of self-imposed lonely days and nights before I got to that point. I hadn't even been able to let my own sister into this frightening new world of mine.

Chapter Sixteen

I awake to the sounds of mournful cries and it takes me a while to realize that they aren't actually mine. It's the cat. I jump from the bed and go searching through the house. I find her at the door of my husband's studio. An audiophile, my husband had a special room built just for listening to his consumer electronics equipment. It's been weeks since he died, but I haven't changed a thing.

"What's the matter little one?" I ask her in soothing tones. "Do you miss him as much as I do?"

I open the door and she races in, running around the room as if looking for him.

Shortly after my husband died, with the cat sleeping by my side, I wondered whether pets experience grief like we do. When she awoke, I went and 'googled' it. And found that cats, in particular, will experience something akin to grief for about six months. I guess that's their short-term memory span. It hasn't been six months yet but I know it will be a lot longer than that before either of us gets over this.

The cat throws herself into a ball on the floor of the studio. I follow suit and together the two of us lay there in despair.

That's when I notice that my husband's computer is on. Nothing surprising there, as I have to leave it on in order to run the wireless network. But the usual screensaver is gone and in its place is a slideshow of photos from our European cruise. One after another, the memories scroll across the screen—their images bright and beckoning in the dim light of the room.

I stare in wonder. Is this the sign? Is my husband trying to tell me something?

But my cat has tired of this visit. She is at the door, mewing insistently once again. Dazed, I follow her out and close the door. I never saw the slideshow appear again, at least on my husband's computer. I ran it plenty of times on my own.

Weeks later, I am sitting in front of his computer once again. The wireless network is down. Nothing I do can get it going again. I have to reboot the computer. The only problem is that I don't know the password.

"Didn't you talk about these things before he died?" my sister asks me incredulously one day when I tell her about my impending fear. "How could you not make sure that this was all written down somewhere?"

In an effort to teach me how to cope when I would be alone, my husband forces me one day to change the filters on our water purification system. We live on well water and use a UV system that requires regular upkeep.

He briefly walks me through the process and I studiously stand by his side taking notes.

The next time it needs to be done, he sends me down to the basement alone to handle the job.

I manage to screw things up. No surprise. Suddenly, there is a torrent of water gushing straight at me. I can't see through my glasses because the stream of water is so strong. My clothes are soaked in a matter of seconds. I try desperately to re-attach the hose I have just unscrewed but the force of the water throws me backwards, never mind getting anywhere close to the actual nozzle.

"Help!" I scream, knowing that my husband is upstairs resting in bed. "Help! Come quickly."

I hear the 'thump' of my husband's cane on the hardwood floors above, a reminder of how frail he has become. It takes a while before he makes his way down the stairs and into the furnace room. By then, there is almost an inch of water on the floor. Everything is sopping wet, including me.

He takes one look at the situation, reaches over and turns off the primary water main that brings water into the house.

"You obviously weren't paying close attention," he observes, before turning around and heading upstairs once again.

We laughed about it for days afterwards. But after he died, I refused to change the filters on my own. I called my father to come do it instead.

"Apple help desk. How can I assist you today?"

I am back in front of my husband's computer with a downed Wi-Fi network.

I explain the situation. My husband has died. The Wi-Fi is down. I need to reboot the computer and I don't know the password.

"No problem dear," says the kind lady sitting God knows how many miles away, probably in some third-world country. "We'll get through this together."

At once, she becomes both a stranger and a friend. I have let my guard down a bit and let her in—I had to in order to explain the situation. And she has embraced me with her tender voice.

She takes me through a series of steps. First, it's a matter of trying to guess his password. After about six or seven attempts of what I think are pretty good guesses, I give up and admit defeat.

"No problem. There's another way around this," the caring and sympathetic voice on the other end of the telephone says. "Do you still have your husband's boot-up disk?"

Technically savvy I am not. That was always my husband's bailiwick so there was no need for me to learn these things. I open his desk drawer, looking for the disk. But all I see are his things. His beloved things. His Mont Blanc pen and the bottles of coloured inks. His stack of business cards. His collection of USB drives (which I will eventually go through one by one in hope of finding something exclusively penned for me). These are things that I know he had cherished.

I break down in tears yet again.

"Don't worry," says the voice. "We're going to get through this together. I am not going to hang up until we have your network up and running again. I will stay on the phone for the next 24 hours if that is what it takes. I can stay here and wait until you are ready to try again. You just give me the word."

It's kind acts like these that make me lose control. I can be strong and determined when I need to be. It's sort of a me-against-the-world type of defiance. It keeps my anger fueled, enough to force me to keep going. But how can I hold onto that defiance when I have someone who is so nice on the other end of the phone, urging me to take my time and assuring me that we will get through this together? She doesn't even know me and yet she has reached out and touched me in a way that has shattered through my emotional barriers.

I'm a wreck.

It's more than a couple of hours later that I finally hang up the phone. She has been as good as her word. The password has been reset—the name of our cat—and the Wi-Fi network is operational once again. All is right with the world, at least with the new world as I now know it.

Chapter Seventeen

It's strange how normal things can change so quickly. One day, we are happily married and living the dream. The next day, we are facing a death sentence.

"You look like you've got the weight of the world on your shoulders," says the President of the Association, one of my communications clients at the time. This is the morning after my husband's diagnosis.

Little does he know that my world has literally changed overnight. And I am still trying to deal with the consequences.

Although both my husband and I go through the next few days in a daze, adhering to normal routines as best we can, neither of us is the same. We may each be coping with the news differently—he by reaching out and telling people of his prognosis and me by withdrawing in until there is nowhere left to go. But we do have each other. And it is this togetherness that gives each of us the strength to carry on.

I may be able to put on a brave front when dealing with the 'outside' world but I come to realize too quickly that it is a very precarious façade.

"Did you know you were going 25 kilometres over the speed limit ma'am?" asks the young police officer who has just pulled me over. I am multi-tasking. Have just dropped off my husband at the local hospital for a blood transfusion and am heading out to buy groceries before I go back to pick him up.

We have been through this routine so often that I have the timing down to a fine art—as long as I put the pedal to the metal.

"I'm sorry officer," I reply. "I'm trying to get back to the hospital in time to pick up my husband."

"Oh, why is he at the hospital?" he queries.

Where do I start? How can I begin to tell this policeman what my life has become?

"He has cancer," I blurt out. "I speed because I drive a lot. I go to four different hospitals in four different cities, depending on the treatment required. There are the blood transfusions, the IV injections, the CAT scans, the infections, the regular check-ups, the emergencies—the list goes on and on. All I seem to do these days is drive."

And with that, I break down in tears and begin sobbing uncontrollably.

Needless to say, he lets me off. But it is a good few minutes before I can pull myself together enough to start driving again.

"You're late," says my husband upon my arrival.

"Yeah, traffic was really bad. There must have been an accident."

No way am I going to let him know about my little meltdown. I have to be strong enough for the two of us.

These little episodes of mine seem to be taking place more and more often. Luckily, they usually occur when I am in the car alone or out on errands on my own. I can't let my husband think that I am not strong enough for him, for us, for the life we now have.

It's during one of our many hospital visits that I find myself losing it yet again. But luckily, it takes place out of his sight.

My husband has gone in for a procedure to implant a Hickman line into his chest (this in addition to the PICC line in his arm that he already has). Both are essentially medical tubes that go directly into the vein; they are often used for blood withdrawal or to administer drugs like antibiotics or chemotherapy. In his case, it will be primarily for dialysis. The waste protein levels in his blood have become too high and his kidneys can no longer function adequately. It means another round of weekly visits to yet another new hospital.

For some reason, this day proves too much for me. It is an additional procedure, one that marks the beginning of another new round of treatment. And it means that my husband's body is beginning to break down. He is getting sicker. As much as the two of us have tried to carry on like all is well and manageable, this is a huge reminder that just the opposite is true.

"I'll wait here," I say to him, as I kiss him goodbye.

I hold it together until they wheel him through the doors. Then I lose it. I try to hold back but try as I might, I can't seem to control anything today, never mind my tears.

I end up curling into a ball on the bench and begin sobbing uncontrollably, almost hysterically if I were to be honest. I know that I have broken every unspoken patient rule by acting out as such but for the life of me, I cannot do anything else but cry.

People walk by and look in. New patients are processed and wheeled in different directions. Efficient hospital workers do what they do on their computers or their phones and feverishly work away. And throughout it all, I continue to bawl.

Part of me wants someone to come over and provide some comfort but the other part of me knows that there is no comfort to be had. It's my burden to carry. Others have their own. And by showing my emotions in such a public manner, I am putting these other people at risk. It's an unspoken rule— and I have broken it.

Finally, after what seems like hours but what I hope are mere minutes, I finally pull it together. My sobbing turns into whimpers. My shaking into controlled breaths.

I pull out my book, begin reading and pretend that nothing ever happened.

"Everything went well," says my husband, when they wheel him back out an hour later.

"I'm glad to hear," I say, willing him not to notice my red eyes and runny nose. "I am so glad."

Chapter Eighteen

Today is the day I have decided to get rid of all my husband's clothes. I have often read of people gathering up their loved one's garments and being able to smell him or her, whatever the case may be. I have tried doing this often, but am unable to summon up his smell.

I open his side of the sliding closet doors, gently gather his suits and jackets and bring them toward my face. I inhale deeply. No. Again, there is nothing.

Like my husband himself, his clothes have already vacated the rich and fulfilling life that they once led.

Before too long, I have amassed a heap of clothes on the bedroom floor. I bring in the green garbage bags and slowly begin the arduous task of saying goodbye.

But there are a few items that I just can't part with—yet. His favourite sweatshirt. His favourite suit jacket. And a couple of T-shirts. Back into the closet they go.

Now that the bags are stuffed, I have an overwhelming desire to be rid of them—immediately. So, I throw them into the car. But as I pull up in front of the town's local clothing box, in creeps a sense of doubt. Should I or shouldn't I? Am I being too hasty? Do I need more time?

"Everyone grieves differently," my sister recently told me. "There is no book of right or wrong. It's a personal process, one that you will have to travel alone."

I think of this now and it gives me the impetus I need to move forward. I toss the bags into the box and head back to the comfort of my home.

The days are long and empty, each one just rolling into the next. I find I am at a loss of what to do with myself. I try reading but my mind wanders. I think of going out but the very thought of interacting with the real world frightens me to no end. I continue to work sporadically but that still leaves me plenty of time with nothing to do.

And so I sit. Waiting for this to be over.

"I'll be there to pick you up at seven," my sister says over the phone, later that day. "A run will do you good. You need to get out and get some fresh air."

My sister and I have been running together for years. My husband never understood the reason why we ran. Just the thought of it, he would say, made him tired.

My husband and I were once in northern Italy on vacation, staying in a beautiful century-old villa that served as a bed and breakfast. I was training for some race and had brought my running shoes and gear with me so that I wouldn't fall too far behind. Every other morning, I would wake early, throw on my shorts and t-shirt, and head into the hills for a run. The lovely Italian couple who owned the place just shook their heads.

"Do you run too?" the gentleman asks my husband one morning during breakfast.

"The only thing that runs on me is my nose," he responds.

Our Italian trip was glorious. It took place well before the days when we knew anything was wrong. It was two weeks filled with ferry trips, car rides and leisurely strolls. It was an endless stream of cafés, cappuccinos and romantic dinners, accompanied by lovely red wines. Everything we could have hoped for and more.

"I'd love to live here for a couple months each year," I confess to my husband one night. We are walking hand-in-hand from the villa to the local restaurant that has become our favourite haunt. "Maybe we could swing this in our retirement. Get away from the harsh winters back home and enjoy this way of life."

"I certainly wouldn't complain if that turned out to be the case," he concurs. "We will definitely have to come back."

I look at the photo taken of the two of us on the outside balcony of the villa during that trip. I see the happy-go-lucky expressions of two people who think their entire lives are still ahead of them. Their dreams and aspirations are well within reach. Their life, they know, is going to be a good one.

But that was not to be.

"How much longer do you think I have?" my husband asks me one day toward the end. "How much longer do you think I will be around?"

Since day one of the diagnosis, I have spent hours and hours online doing research on his disease. I have joined forums, associations and groups. Have attended seminars. Queried specialists. Spoken to others with the disease and tried to amass as much information as I could.

I know that the latest cocktail of drugs isn't working. Have seen the blood results. I realize that there are only a few options left. But I can't let him down. I have to keep that hope alive.

"I think that once we start the next round of drugs, things will improve," I reply. "I think we've got lots of time left. No need to start worrying yet."

Chapter Nineteen

We're in Chicago. We've come with my sister and her husband for another one of our much-needed breaks. It's been a gruelling round of treatment as of late. Nothing seems to be working and we're both getting edgy.

"We're just heading off for four days," I say to the oncologist. "We will be back next week, in time for the next round of treatment."

"I don't think you should go," he states. "It's too risky. Your husband is not in the best of health."

I stop in my tracks momentarily. This is the same oncologist who told us months ago to go ahead with our planned trip to Berlin—the last trip to Berlin as it turned out. I was the one hesitant at the time. My husband was pushing for it and I was holding back.

"Go and have yourself a great time," he said. "Everything will be fine. Enjoy it."

And here he is telling us that a short jaunt to the U.S. is a no-no.

Despite his warnings, we go ahead with the trip. And we have a wonderful 'vacation'.

Sure, there were a couple of alarming moments. Like the time my husband wasn't feeling well and we had to call back home to ask our pharmacist for advice. Yeah, he was a bit shocked to get our call but he dutifully made some queries and called us back with a suggested mix of medications that we had fortunately brought with us.

Let's hear it for cell phones. And dedicated pharmacists.

My husband and I lived just outside of a very small town. Our pharmacy was the only one available and it prided itself on delivering individual customer care.

It isn't long after my husband's diagnosis that I begin making the regular trips to the pharmacy. It had been relatively mundane medications prior to this, like birth control, antibiotics, whatever. These latest drugs are decidedly different.

I am still in a state of shock and barely manage to hand over the prescriptions. The pharmacist must know something is up but he never wavers in his friendly demeanour. Never asks a personal question. Never takes me to task on how my husband's health is.

It's small gestures like this for which I remain eternally grateful; they're the ones that enable me to get through the nightmare. One day at a time. One moment at a time.

Eventually, I am able to make mention of the disease and the pharmacist takes his cues accordingly.

At one point, one of the newly ordered prescriptions we need comes at a cost of $1,000. I actually burst into tears. It is the 'straw' that breaks the camel's back that day. It is a different one on different days. But the straws keep adding up and, sooner or later, I just can't hold it together anymore and the camel inevitably collapses.

"I think this company has a patient-assistance program," says the pharmacist, while I stand there mute, with tears running down my face. "Let me get them on the phone for you."

A series of questions later and the fee has been reduced to $200. I have learned my lesson this time around and fudged the financials.

"Don't worry about it right now," says the pharmacist, when I try to exchange my VISA for the pills. "We'll catch you next time."

He never did charge me.

Chapter Twenty

I've taken to having conversations with my husband, even though he's been dead for several months now. Sometimes it's in the car, when I'm driving to visit a family member. That's pretty much the only place I go these days. Sometimes it's in the house. It's become more frequent as of late, as if I am getting frustrated with his lack of response.

I know in my head that my husband is dead. But 20+ years is a long time and, in my heart, he is still very much alive.

"We're holding a memorial for you next week," I say to him one morning. "I think you'll be happy with it. We've invited your work mates, as well as our friends of course."

My sister has once again stepped up to the plate and arranged everything on my behalf. She found the restaurant, decided upon the time, the food, the beverages—everything that needed to be done, she did it.

I choose my attire with care. Not black—that's too much. Everyone will expect that. Not something bright. That would be garish. It has to be subtle but simple. I feel like I am going to be put on display. That people will want to see how the new widow is doing. I recently had to fill out a dentist form of some sort and checked the 'widow' box for the first time. That was an eye-opener. Hadn't even realized it was an option until then.

I've chosen a light grey dress and black heels. I am wearing a matching set of earrings and a necklace—one that my husband had bought for me on one of our many business/pleasure trips. I am also wearing my husband's wedding ring. Mine lay in my bedside table. This is my way of telling him that he will be with me forever—regardless of what has happened.

A few weeks after my husband died, I was out swimming laps in the backyard pool. It was just the monotonous sort of thing that helped me cope with the loss, forcing my head to count instead of remember.

While in the midst of these laps, I felt my engagement ring fly off my hand and sail over my head. I was beside myself with worry. Spent two hours searching the pool, walking from one end to the other over and over, and then over again. In a panic, I went inside the house, telephoned my neighbour, and begged him to come help me search for it. The thought of losing that ring was killing me. My husband had lovingly scrimped and saved to buy it. He had it designed just for me. As hokey as it sounds, it is still a symbol of our love. I just wouldn't be able to cope if I had lost it.

After another futile couple of hours, my neighbour gave up in defeat. I, too, was weary and exhausted by this time. I thanked him for his efforts and, as I turned to lock the gate, I noticed something sparkling in the long grass beside the fence. I bent down to pick it up and there was my engagement ring. I sighed with relief and made a promise to myself to get all of my rings resized the next day.

"So what do you think?" I ask my husband—inside my head this time, as there are people walking about during the memorial. "Are you okay with this?"

He doesn't reply. Actually, he never does. But the night goes as smoothly as can be expected. I interact with everyone. Make a point of speaking to one and all. It is like being at a press event, with my husband confidently standing by my side. Except no one can see him—not even me. But I know he is there nonetheless.

Of course, the endless supply of red wine does a lot to help my demeanour throughout the evening. It isn't too long before I am out in the parking lot with the rest of the 'outcasts', bumming cigarettes off anyone who will give me one.

It has been years since the two of us stopped smoking. I was first and my husband followed a couple years later. We joked about what we would do with all the money we would save as a result but that never seemed to happen.

Unfortunately, the urge to smoke has once again reared its ugly head.

"I think everything went well," I mention to my friend on the phone a few days later, my throat still raw from the self-imposed abuse. "I think he would have liked it, had he been there. Of course, it's a shame that his boss couldn't attend. After all the years that he worked for them."

That still irked me. My husband and I had spent many evenings with the boss and his wife. We always met up at trade shows or other media events. And we made it a point to meet regularly in town as well. They were away in Florida, which is understandable. But they had had more than three months to come back for the memorial as a sign of respect. I would have done it if the shoe had been on the other foot.

"Luckily, I didn't let on about my disappointment on that front," I say to my friend.

"Oh, but you did," she replies. "You made your feelings very well known to the boss' son. In fact, you were more than clear on how you felt about the situation."

Oops. I never was good at getting office politics right. I guess all of that wine opened a few wounds, more than I wanted to admit. But there was nothing I could do about it now. The cat was out of the bag.

Months afterward, I learn that my husband's boss has screwed him, or rather, screwed me. Promises made to entice my husband to stay onboard during hard times in his 30 years of service turn out to be mere words. Years later, I am happy to hear that the company has filed for bankruptcy. What goes around, comes around. Or that's what they say anyway.

People also talk about karma, as if there is some almighty being standing on top of the world keeping count with a large scroll—or maybe an iPad in this day and age. It's all rubbish. There is no karma. There is no 'life is fair'.

My husband was the kindest, nicest and funniest man I knew. He was, by far, a better person than me. Of all people who deserved to live a long and healthy life, he topped the list.

But he didn't get that. He was chopped down in life at the young age of 58—a man still in his prime. And I had been left adrift. Maybe his death was actually meant as a punishment for me—to make me suffer for my vices. But if that's the case, then how cruel a world it is.

Chapter Twenty-One

It's the morning after the memorial service. I am slightly hung-over. No surprise there. My intake of wine has increased significantly since my husband's death.

"A glass of wine helps take the edge off," I try to explain to my mother. "It lets me relax just enough so that I can cope."

"Well, that certainly doesn't sound good," she replies, having not had a drink herself in more than a few decades. "And I don't know what you mean about having to take the edge off. The edge off what?"

Sometimes you can't see the forest for the trees.

The memorial had taken place months after my husband's death. I planned it that way intentionally.

"I am so sick of this winter," my husband says one afternoon, shortly before his death. We are both lying in bed, watching TV—he with his notebook computer on his lap as usual. He had been bedridden for a few weeks. A misstep in the house led to a broken ankle which then gave root to a serious infection that kept him off his feet.

"I just want to see the sun again, to see spring," he continues, longingly gazing out of our bay window to the snow-covered fields that lay beyond. "Is that too much to ask?"

In fact, it is one of only a few things that he asks for during his illness. He is forever appreciative of the smallest gesture or the simplest kindness. He constantly bends over backwards to assure everyone that everything is fine.

My husband ends up dying on a cold, wintry day in March. The sun hadn't appeared in some time. But on the day that follows, it shines so brightly that the snow seems to sparkle and glisten all on its own. I cry over the injustice of my husband not living to see it.

It is then that I decide my husband will have sunshine during his memorial. And thus, the date is set.

In a way, the time preceding the event gives me something to aim towards. It is terrifying yet necessary. But as the day draws closer and closer, I become less and less sure that I will be able to attend.

"You don't have to show up," my sister reassures me. "If you can't do it, you can't do it. No one is going to think less of you for feeling like you do."

But, of course, I have to do it. And as the day approaches and the people come through the door, I stand tall and hold it together—all for the sake of my husband.

Now that the memorial is over, I feel adrift in a torrent of emotions. My husband has officially been 'remembered'. People have come to pay their respects. And now, everyone is moving on with their lives. Except for me.

I spend my time back at the house, whiling away the hours by pouring over old photos and wallowing in the emptiness of it all.

The one constant through all of this is my family. My mother and sister slowly cajole me into leaving the house more often and 're-entering' the real world. My mother takes to bringing me weekly supplies of chocolate-covered jujubes—one of the few things I can actually eat. But even her hopes are out of line. At one point, I must have a few kilograms of them in the cupboard. And still she brings more.

It's not only me that feels the ache of loss over my husband's death. As painful as it is, it's good to know that others are still thinking of him, are continuing to mourn him— even as time goes on.

Sometimes I just sit in the car in the parking lot and cry. But there are other days when I can actually get out with my mother or my sister, or both of them, and walk into a store or grab a cup of coffee.

It is during these times that I realize I have been using my grief like a warm blanket on a winter's night to keep others out so that I could avoid reality. It is my solitude. My suffering. My life that is over. But the point is that this is my new reality. As painful as it is, it is the only one I have. Ahead of me are two choices: to join my husband or to continue forward on my own.

The fact that my sister and husband were so close provides deep solace to me. It isn't uncommon for the two of us to get caught up in our grief together. And it is my sister who eventually helps me find the strength to go on.

She often accompanied me and my husband on our weekend-shopping jaunts or travels. We regularly visited the spa—staying overnight to gain the full benefit of a relaxing get-away.

My sister even joins us, one time, on our annual business trip to Vegas. The fire alarm at the hotel sounds during the night and it is all she can do to rouse the two of us from our bed.

"I looked in the hall and it's all white out there. I think it's smoke," she screams. "Come on, we have to go. Now."

My husband and I slowly come awake but take a bit of time to understand the seriousness of the situation. It is while we are still grappling with it that we get dressed and grab our belongings, at least those we value the most.

"We don't have time for this. Let's go now," my sister urges.

As we follow the seemingly endless stream of people down the 17 flights of stairs, we each give thanks for being able to get out safely. But once we get down to the parking lot and eventually into the lobby, we find that no one there knows anything about the alarm. Turns out someone pulled the lever and let loose with the fire hose. It is an isolated event. A prank.

Luckily for us, we are compensated for our midnight misadventure with a credit at the hotel restaurant and gift shop. But, because we are leaving the next day, we have no easy way to spend it. All three of us, however, are 'junk-food-oholics' so we turn the credit into assorted bags of chips and candy for our carry-on luggage. The plane ride home the following day turns out to be a decadently delightful one.

My sister and I periodically convinced my husband to join us for a weekend get-away at a nearby spa, located about a 45-minute drive away from our house. We girls would opt for the mani and pedi, followed by an hour-long massage. My husband would choose the gentleman's facial before his massage. He would be in seventh heaven.

It was after one of these weekend get-aways that my husband decided to purchase one of the resort's luxurious spa housecoats as one of my Christmas presents. He drove back to the spa the following week, walked into reception, made his purchase and was on his way back to the car.

"I was thinking about what a great time we had just had there," he told me later. "I was reminiscing about how wonderful everything was."

Unknown to my husband or sister—so they tell me—my sister was coincidently at the same resort on the same day for a business conference. She was on her way back from a bathroom break and happened to glance out of the window. Apparently, she couldn't believe it when she saw my husband in the parking lot, so she ran outside, calling his name.

And thus, their little secret was born. Both swore to say nothing of the encounter for fear of giving away the Christmas present. Each acted like a little kid, with a silly grin on his face in the knowledge of their shared secret. I knew something was up but no amount of pleading on my part could get either to confess.

The day after my husband and I exchanged our Christmas presents, my sister was one of the first to call.

"Has he told you yet?" she gleefully inquired. "You cannot believe how badly we both wanted to tell you the story. It's taken all of our will power to keep it from you."

My sister has always played a huge role in my life—in both the good and bad times. It was so heartening to hear of a little drama shared just between the two of them.

It is comforting to know, in a way, that I am not the only one who misses him. And my sister proves to be a godsend when things take a turn.

Chapter Twenty-Two

There were many times during my marriage when my sister and I would go shopping for the day. More often than not, my husband was happy to join us. But he rarely followed us into the clothing boutiques, opting instead to peruse the audio-video stores or anything similar which would catch his fancy. This often led to unconventional ways of finding each other, like being in a change-room only to hear him bellow: "Polar Bear, are you in there? Polar Bear, can you hear me?"

I would sheepishly answer or shyly emerge out of the fitting room, embarrassed by what the clerks could be thinking. I always imagined them visualizing some thickset, overweight person. Someone maybe weighing 300 pounds. I am sure that more than one shopper let her imagination run wild when she heard the nickname.

Let's face it, it's not a very complimentary one. But once my husband was onto something, he stuck with it.

Years earlier, I had travelled up to Yellowknife with a girlfriend. The son of the innkeeper where we stayed told me that I walked like a polar bear. It should come as no surprise to learn that I didn't think of this as a compliment.

When my husband and I got together, I happened to mention this to him and the nickname stuck. Things seemed to snowball from there and eventually, our house became the 'Bear Lair'—filled with every kind of 'bearaphernalia' imaginable.

We had polar bear plates, mugs, platters, duvet covers— the list went on and on. After my husband died, I slowly began sifting through this collection—readying myself for the time to pare it down. But before his death, it had become almost an obsession for the both of us.

During my marriage, there were very few occasions—if any—that my husband used my proper name, opting for the nickname instead. He eventually extended this nicknaming to my entire family so that my mother became 'Mama Bear', my dad 'Mr. Bear', and so on and so on. Even my cousins and aunts were not immune.

Initially, everyone took it in great fun. But eventually, it became almost a badge of honour for us. We each had been deemed 'special' in our own personal way. And somehow, over time, it just became accepted. We even began substituting our proper names with our new monikers amongst ourselves.

During his constant search for new polar bears to add to our collection, my husband stumbles upon a line of sculptures done by a Canadian artist. We are beside ourselves with excitement. Not only is there an entire collection to be had but each piece in the collection is done to perfection—every nuance finished perfectly in homage to the majestic strength of polar bears in the wild.

The sculptures are expensive but my husband surprises me one Christmas with a large, upright one entitled 'Dancing Bear'.

"It's in honour of you," he tells me that night. "You love to dance."

Eventually, the collection grows and soon, we're ordering a beautiful custom corner cabinet to house them all.

The Christmas after my husband's diagnosis, my husband presents me with yet another poignant piece, this one of a polar bear standing erect, his front paws pressed together in prayer.

"It's called 'The Believer'," he informs me. "I thought you would like it."

Oh how I wished for the magic of that sculpture to rub off on us. At that point, we were down but not yet defeated. Yes, he had been given the prognosis. But no, neither of us wanted to believe it to be true.

"It's not a death sentence," the oncologist says. "A lot of people with multiple myeloma end up living a very long time."

This is the second oncologist we are consulting. We wanted another opinion and sought out an alternate specialist in the field. And it is before we know about the chromosomal abnormality that will shorten my husband's life expectancy to three years.

"It's amazing what modern science and the human body can do," he continues. "I have this one patient who had Stage 4 breast cancer. We tried everything but there was nothing we could do to stop it. Eventually, the cancer spread to her brain and she was advised to get her affairs in order. Then one day, she says she's feeling better. And the same thing happens the next day and the next. And she is looking better. Is eating. Is walking. Joking. So we take some MRIs and CAT scans, and sure enough, there is no sign of the cancer. We check again and we can't see it anywhere. It's a miracle if there ever was one. So the moral of this is not to give up hope. Keep believing and you just never know what may happen."

Well, despite our best efforts, the worst has happened. But I still gaze at 'The Believer' in wonderment. Maybe there is some way to unleash its powers. Or maybe it's a matter of choosing what you believe in. I, for one, believe that my husband remains with me, even to this day. Maybe that's where the power of belief can take hold.

Chapter Twenty-Three

On our tenth wedding anniversary, my husband and I splurge on a trip to Churchill, Manitoba, to see the polar bears. We catch the plane to Winnipeg before continuing on to Churchill itself. Once there, we stay at a small inn, sharing a tiny bed and a communal bathroom. Not your Ritz-Carlton, that's for sure. But we happily make it our home for the week, going out on the tundra buggies every day to see the great white majestic beasts up close and personal.

My husband takes his camera equipment with him on these daily treks. He bops from seat to seat on the buggie, trying to capture this or that polar bear in the best light. By the second day, we've made friends with the other polar bear 'aficionados' and they happily move out of the way to accommodate him.

Later, my husband will print out the better of these photos and use them to adorn the walls of our house. One, in particular, shows a polar bear standing erect, with his front paws and head against the driver's window of another buggy. It's a great shot of us and them—together and yet not together.

It is while we are in Churchill that we feel truly at home. Just like our own humble abode, every inn, restaurant and store is decorated with polar bear knick-knacks and wall coverings. Everywhere you look has the polar bear theme done to the nines. We are ecstatically happy in these surroundings, pulling out the credit cards to add to our collection—a rare feat, considering that my husband has already used all the resources of the Internet to create quite an impressive array of polar bear collectibles.

The trip turns out to be one of the more memorable ones for us. And we manage to come home with our bags stuffed to the brim with polar bear items to help fill in the gaps in our growing collection.

Our house has become an homage to polar bears. People—the few who enter our doors—take to calling us eccentric. They roll their eyes or gasp at the sheer breadth of it all.

But to us, it's become ordinary. We get a friend to paint our guest bathroom in a huge, three-dimensional polar bear mural that covers the entire four walls and ceiling. We finish the room off with a polar bear tiffany lamp, a gift from my husband's mother, who has also eagerly 'bought' into our theme.

We add in a mixture of sculptures, plush toys, blankets, window coverings, towels and even soap dispensers. There is too much to mention. And too much to take in all at once for the uninitiated. But to us, it's normal.

We eventually purchase a hot tub, one in which we can delight in the control pad that prominently features the company's polar bear logo.

Today, I continue to take solace in these surroundings. The bears stand tall and proud, wherever you look. They remain a reflection of us, of what we had together and how we were able to create this special place.

Chapter Twenty-Four

It's a new day. The memorial service is now weeks behind me. I feel like I have made a huge step forward. I must be getting stronger. After all, it's been almost four months.

The summer has come on in full swing. The weather is warm. The birds are chirping. It is one of those days where my husband and I would have just jumped in the car, gone for a drive and seen where the road took us.

I have been toying with the idea of going to visit my sister for the past few days. She lives a couple hours away and I haven't seen her in a bit so I am planning to stay the night.

Fortunately, I like to drive. I haven't called her to see if she will be home because I really haven't decided for sure.

So, I get in the car. I insert a CD—Bruckner's *Symphony #7*, performed by the Berlin Philharmonic— and off I go. It's my husband's favourite symphony and I can't help but feel close to him as I hear the opening plaintive notes take hold.

My husband and I had made this trek a hundred times. But he always drove. He loved driving.

"Have you ever noticed that there are never any police at the top of hills?" he asks me one day.

My husband loved to speed. He would go 170 kilometres while on major highways—but only while going uphill. Once he reached the peak, he would take his foot off the pedal and coast.

And he was a polite driver, always willing to take his turn at the front of the pack to bear the risk of being caught by any potential police car waiting in the wings. We'd often travel with two or three other like-minded drivers, each taking his turn dutifully before falling back into the safety of the pack. In this way, we would reach my sister's house in record time.

Today, it is just me. And my CD. And quite a few tears.

By the time I reach my sister's, I am a bit of a wreck. Very anxious about being so far away from my safe haven and worried about the pets. Are they okay? Do they need me?

This is my first 'major' solo trip since my husband's death. And I am not handling it all that well.

"Hi," my sister says, after opening the door and seeing it is me. There aren't any huge exclamations or over-the-top greetings. For me to show up unannounced, especially at this juncture in my life, is a highly unusual event. But my sister takes it all in stride and keeps it low-key—just what I need.

"What a nice surprise. Do you want to come in for a cup of coffee?"

I had rigged up a camera at home so I could monitor my house with my iPhone. The first thing I do at my sister's is check to see if the pets are okay. But no matter how hard I try, I can't get the connection to work.

My husband and I had used this technology many times before. We would be in Savannah or San Francisco and gleefully peer in to see how the cats and the parrot were doing, whether they were becoming anxious in our absence. When we were away, my mother would often take on the pet-sitting duties. She had never been around birds before but had adapted rather well when we introduced the newcomer to the family.

"Gramma," she cooed, lingering over the word while holding the parrot on her fingers. "Gramma." But try as she might, for years to come, she never got the parrot to mimic her.

My husband and I would laugh with my mother during these times. We would also caution her about our ability to peer electronically into the bedroom while we were away, joking that she should be careful of what she did there or with whom.

Once, when we were in Europe, we turned on this technology only to discover a large, hand-written sign that read: 'We Miss You'.

My mother has her own sense of humour, it seems.

But today, here at my sister's, I spend a frustrating few minutes grappling with this technology before realizing that I am not going to get it to work, no matter how hard I try. My husband was always the technically proficient one, not me.

If I can't see home, then I need to get home. Quickly.

My sister, again, is ever reasonable.

"Don't worry if you need to go," she says, seeing my anxiety increase. "It was nice of you to come all this way for a visit. But I totally understand if you can't stay."

I bid a hasty, teary goodbye and make my way back home. Too soon. I'm not ready yet.

But I had made the effort. That should count for something, shouldn't it?

As I make my way back, I am amazed at how something that seemed so easy all these years has proven to be so difficult for me now. It's almost like having to learn to walk again, after being stricken down by a stroke. It's about learning how to live on your own again. And it's hard.

Chapter Twenty-Five

My sister and I are with my father. We're travelling away for the weekend to visit a friend of his, a friend of the family actually.

This is the first time I have left my husband alone for any length of time since the diagnosis. I had hemmed and hawed but finally had been convinced to go.

"You need some time off," my sister inveigles. "You've been running around at breakneck speed for months now and one of these days, you're just going to collapse and then what will the two of you do? You need to get away—for yourself."

And so, I have come. With strict instructions for my husband to call me regularly, to let me know he is doing alright in my absence.

It's the morning after we left. My husband and I spoke on the phone the night before and all seemed well. My father, sister and I are staying at a little dive of a motel. It was all that we could find on this seemingly deserted island but hey, it's an adventure, right?

There seems to be an entire motorcycle gang that is after this same adventure and 'luckily', they are all staying at the same 'quaint', little motel.

Needless to say, my sister and I are being extra cautious to avoid eye contact with any of the men—or women for that matter.

There is a dampness in the air but my sister, wont as she is to keep me moving, insists on going out for a run. We don our shorts and T's, put on our running shoes, and head out.

The dampness turns into a light drizzle and before too long, the drizzle becomes a steady torrent of rain. I can't see through my glasses, and my sister kindly gives me her cap so I can at least try to follow her to the motel.

We are halfway back when we see headlights approaching. In fact, they're coming right at us. We both begin cursing the recklessness of drivers as the vehicle continues directly toward us.

Just as we are about to be swept off to the side of the road, the vehicle stops. The window lowers and my father's worried face peers out.

"I didn't know if it was safe for you girls and I was concerned about the weather. Do you want to hop in and I can take you back?"

What are fathers for?

My sister and I still fondly recall the story to this day.

After everyone is back safe and sound at the motel (and dry), I make the call to my husband. There is no answer. I'm okay with that. Maybe he slept in. Is in the washroom. Listening to music. Who knows?

We go down to breakfast, which consists of a coffee and a stale muffin. Once we're back in the room, I try calling a second time.

Again, no answer.

"I'm sure he's fine," says my sister. "You know him. He gets caught up in something and doesn't even hear the phone."

We head off to visit my father's friend and I am making calls every hour on the hour.

Finally, I break down and telephone my neighbour. I explain the situation, beg him to go over and make sure my husband is okay.

He calls back within a few minutes.

"I found him outside fixing the riding lawnmower," he reports. "He's got pieces of it all over your back lawn. Says he's busy and he'll call you later."

Relief floods through me. He is fine. He is, in fact, his old self it would seem. Too preoccupied to deal with little things, like calling his wife regularly to let her know he's okay.

Yeah, my husband may be sick and dying but he is still very much the same man I married.

Chapter Twenty-Six

My husband and I are in Europe. We're packing, getting ready to head home after a delightful two-week holiday. I've got my passport in hand and am eager to go.

But my husband refuses to budge. He is just sitting there on the bed, staring at me.

"Let's go," I say. "The cab is going to be here any minute."

"I can't find my passport," he replies.

I am starting to get angry. Here we are thousands of miles away from home. The flight is imminent, and he hasn't even started packing yet. Nor does he know where his passport is. We have obligations back home. There are the pets that my mother is minding. We have work to do. Doctor appointments to fulfill. A myriad of responsibilities.

"What do you mean you can't find it? What did you do with it? When was the last time you saw it? And why aren't you busy packing?"

This continues for another ten minutes before I startle myself awake and realize it's all been a dream.

I find myself dreaming of my husband almost every night. It's actually a welcome relief to get to the end of the day and slip into our time together. It's like we're continuing to be married but in another dimension.

I've heard a lot of people say they often think they see their loved one in a crowd or on a familiar street. Just a quick glimpse, but they're positive it's him or her. They rush over, sometimes even pulling on an arm or shoulder, only to discover they are wrong. That's when they realize that their loved ones are actually dead and that they won't ever see them again.

I wait for this to happen to me in the months afterward. But it never does.

Maybe this is what I get instead. All of these lovely dreams where we get to spend time together. Lately, however, these welcome episodes are ending on a bit of a sour note—like the lost passport or the refusal to leave a hotel room—but at least we're together again. I don't have any difficulties in remembering my husband's face. I see him almost every night in my dreams.

"Do you think this means that I'm stuck in reliving the past?" I ask my sister one night. We're both enjoying a glass of wine at her house. I have managed to make it there—successfully this time.

"I think there isn't any script of where you should or shouldn't be," she replies. "You are where you need to be to get through this."

Prescient words, ones that would stay with me a long time.

It is my sister whom I called that last night at the hospital. My husband had been experiencing stomach pains for most of the evening. They were getting progressively worse.

"I'm going to call the ambulance," I finally say. "Something is wrong."

It is the first time I have ever called 911.

"Fire. Police. Ambulance?"

"Ambulance," I reply, trying to steady the tremor in my voice.

They are there in less than ten minutes.

"You're coming with me, aren't you?" my husband pleads, as the two attendants whisk him into the waiting vehicle.

I want to join him in the ambulance but am not allowed, so I follow in my car instead. We get to the hospital at around ten at night.

We are admitted into emergency after just a few minutes. A nurse comes in and hooks him up to a series of monitors. Blood is drawn. And then we wait.

After what seems like an eternity, the doctor comes in to tell us that it is just a minor infection. He will prescribe antibiotics and all will be fine. But he wants to keep my husband overnight for observation, given his condition.

It is after midnight when I kiss my husband good-bye, tell him I will be back first thing in the morning, and begin my drive home.

When I enter the house, the phone is already ringing.

"This is the nurse from the hospital," the voice intones. "You need to get back here right away."

By the time I arrive, there is a full-on medical team working on him. He is barely conscious but I manage to tell him that I am there, by his side. He opens his eyes to acknowledge me and then drifts off again. It isn't too long after, that they take him away for a whole barrage of tests and procedures.

And it is a couple hours later that the chief doctor comes in to tell me the news. He isn't going to make it this time. They are doing all they can to make him comfortable. Do I have anyone I could call to be with me?

It is 3:00 in the morning.

My husband and I have already discussed this possibility. He made me promise that it would be just the two of us. He didn't want anyone remembering him in any way other than his normal self.

I feel bound to respect his wish but I also feel like I have to let someone know. This is serious. The family should be told.

After much deliberation, I call my sister but hang up after two rings. It can wait until later in the morning.

"Is everything okay?" she asks, phoning me back within seconds. "I'm sorry I missed your call."

She is on her way in minutes. And it is she whom I join in the waiting room shortly after they unplug my husband from life support.

The date is March 11, 2011. The same day as the Japanese earthquake and tsunami, which killed more than 15,000 people.

My husband always did like to do things large.

Chapter Twenty-Seven

The months pass and I realize that I still need to make good on my promise. My sister and I are in Berlin, staying at the same little hotel where my husband and I always stayed when we were visiting. We are in town only for a few days, long enough to visit the city and to take in the Berlin Philharmonic. The orchestra is performing Bruckner's *Symphony # 7*.

I've tucked a couple of handfuls of my husband's ashes in a bundle of tissues and have dutifully carried them across borders and time zones. I know it's illegal, but I had promised him after all. My sister knows the reason for my visit and has agreed to accompany me. Thank God for my sister.

Of course, getting the ashes themselves wasn't quite as easy as I thought it would be. They had been safely ensconced in a plain wooden box for the past few months, with a brass name plate bearing witness to 'who' was inside—as if I would ever forget.

It is a beautiful summer afternoon when I decide to take the box out of the bedroom and onto the back patio. It comes as a bit of a surprise to discover that it doesn't open easily. There is no clasp or lock that I can detect. It looks, for all intents and purposes, like the seal is never meant to be broken.

But that just won't do. So, I go into the kitchen and get a knife, more determined than ever to crack open that box and retrieve a few ashes for the trip. After numerous tries, all I have are deep gashes in the wood to mark my many futile attempts. But I am not one to give up. Where there is a will, there is a way.

A couple of hours later, I am exhausted—physically and emotionally. And I am stumped. Short of actually getting a saw and cutting through the wood, I can detect no way of getting my hands on the ashes. Does this mean that my husband doesn't really want to go?

"Let's face it, I'm not going to ever get back to Berlin," he says to me one night, a few weeks before he died. We had our trip booked for a couple of months and then he stumbled one day and broke his ankle. The drugs had taken their toll on both his immune system and his bones.

The break became infected and what was bad ended up getting much, much worse. But throughout it all, he held fast to the notion that he would get better, at least better enough to make it to Berlin one last time.

We made arrangements to postpone the trip by a couple of months and kept our fingers crossed. And we waited and hoped.

"Don't talk like that," I reply. "Of course, we will make it back there. At least once more."

But it was not to going to happen. My husband died a few weeks later of septic shock. The trip was postponed yet again. It would eventually be just my sister and me.

In the meantime, I still have this damn wooden box to deal with. I go down into the basement to retrieve the handsaw, and only when I turn the box over to begin sawing do I see the four tiny screws hidden on the bottom. Note to all: always turn the box over to see what's on the other side.

Within seconds, I have the screws out and the bag of ashes open. I take out a couple of handfuls and put the rest back— saving them for another day when I would sprinkle them on the grounds of our property.

"Do you want to come with me when I scatter your mom's ashes?" I gently queried my husband, years before. His sister had asked me if I minded taking care of this last request of her mother. I assured her that I would be honoured to take on the task, never realizing that I would one day be doing the same with her brother.

"No, I have no desire to join you," my husband replied. "Although I'm glad that you're doing it for my sister."

So, I headed out on my own. After what I felt was a suitable but respectful moment of silence, I opened the bag and began trickling the ashes out onto the ground. But soon broke into a coughing spell instead. Turns out the wind was stronger than I had anticipated and almost all of what I was sprinkling ended up being blown back into my face.

I re-entered the house covered with ashes from head to toe. My husband was on the floor laughing hysterically. He had witnessed the entire episode from the window.

I had learned my lesson. So, when the time came for me to scatter the balance of my husband's ashes, I made sure that the winds were minimal. And I met with much better success the second go around.

But right now, I am in the lobby of the Berliner Philharmonie with the tissue of ashes safely hidden in my purse.

"I am in desperate need of a glass of wine," I say to my sister, who kindly proceeds to get me one.

We stand at the tall cocktail tables looking around and trying to avoid the subject of how I am going to get my husband's ashes onto the concert-hall stage. I have been mulling it over for several nights and think I have figured out a plan. But I am already feeling the heady emotions of grief and fear, and don't know if I have the courage to go through with it.

We eventually finish our wine and make our way into the hall. The first half of the concert is some modern classical piece that I do not know, and I am thankful when the intermission finally arrives.

Now's my time to act. I get up and, instead of following the crowd into the lobby, make my way to the balcony that hangs over the right side of the stage. By the time I get there, there are but a few people left in the area.

"You can't do this," my sister pleads. She has turned traitor since arriving in the hall. "You'll get arrested and end up in jail. He would never have wanted that. You have to stop. Let's go get another glass of wine instead."

Frightened and emotional, I turn to my sister and sternly inform her that she is more than welcome to leave but that I have to go through with this. She steadfastly stands by my side.

With shaking fingers, I dig into my purse and grab the tissue. I try nonchalantly to bring my hand to the balcony railing. I take one last furtive look around and unravel the tissue. The ashes make a small arc as they float to the stage below. I've done it.

"Let's get out of here. Now," pleads my sister. "Come on. Let's go."

We make it to the lobby and I greedily inhale a glass of wine. My sister has chosen to abstain this time around. So, I gulp down her glass as well.

We head back into the hall and I can't help but notice that the Double Bass player on the right opts to discreetly wipe off his chair before he sits. And I smile.

But that smile instantly turns into tears as soon as I hear the slow, plaintive notes of the opening score. The tears only get worse as the performance progresses, as if my emotions are rising and falling with the notes themselves. And then the floodgates open and I can't hold back. My sister reaches out and grabs my hand. But that only brings more tears.

Thankfully, there are no police waiting to arrest us at the end of the concert. And there are no recriminations from my sister. And best of all, it is done. I wonder if my husband is there with me in Berlin, if he can travel as easily—or more easily—than I can.

"I'm sure that the person beside you thought you were really moved by the performance," my sister remarks later, when we are safely back at the hotel.

All that night, I am kept awake by the certainty that my husband will give me a sign to acknowledge my efforts. I have fulfilled his last request. I have gotten him to the Berliner Philharmonie one last time. I am deserving of a sign, aren't I? How hard can it be?

I recall reading somewhere that after someone dies, his spirit stays for only a short period of time before moving on. When I had visited the fortune teller on that traumatic day so soon after my husband's death, I remember her saying that he had been caught by surprise and that he wasn't ready to move on, that he wanted to stay close by instead. But it's been months now. So maybe he has come to terms with his situation. Regardless, I lay awake all night. But I don't receive a sign.

The next day, I feel drained—physically and emotionally. It's like I have taken three steps back instead of one step forward. But it's time to go home. I have to say goodbye to Berlin—and to the part of my husband that I have lovingly left behind.

Chapter Twenty-Eight

Shortly after we were married, I began asking my husband if we could get a dog. We lived in the middle of nowhere so had plenty of room for one. We each had dogs when we were young and were both big animal lovers.

In fact, there were many times throughout our marriage when we would endeavour to save the little field mice who would mistakenly scurry into our house for safety and warmth only to discover our cats instead.

"Grab the kitchen strainer," my husband would holler. "They have another one."

Inevitably, we would catch the little critters, tuck them into a box of some sort and drive them to a nearby field. I would stand at the window and wave goodbye as my husband drove off, little field mouse by his side on the passenger seat.

We also had bats, birds, squirrels and chipmunks in the house. Not at the same time, thank goodness. And always, we did our best to catch them and bring them to safety. The bats and birds were tricky, as they were exceedingly hard to catch. Usually, we would just try to shepherd them toward the open patio doors.

But the squirrels proved the most difficult of all. We'd listen to them rattling about in the attic and wonder what they were up to—dreading the appearance of babies. Eventually, we ended up coercing a friend to tackle the job for us. When the day came, the three of us anxiously waited outside in strategic positions, on watch to see the little critter make his graceful exit from the rooftop. And then my husband and I gaped in wonder as our friend hastily climbed the two-storey ladder and plugged the hole where the squirrel had just exited.

What a relief! The end of what could have proven to be a disaster.

But alas, later that night, we hear the now familiar scurrying once again. We make the requisite phone call and the next morning, the three of us are once again strategically placed around the house—on watch for the second entrance that we had missed the first time around.

With both of us being huge animal lovers, the thought of adding a dog to our family seems like a perfect idea to me.

But my husband resists.

"We travel too much. And we don't have anyone to take care of the pets," he says.

My mother would often babysit our pets but a dog would be a lot more responsibility than cats and a parrot. She would have to stay at our house for days at a time.

I explain that my sister has dogs and would no doubt be glad to mind ours when the need arose. She later verifies that this is the case.

But still he resists.

Years later, in a moment of exasperation, I blurt out that I will be getting a dog as soon as he is gone. Words that, to this day, I regret. He takes it all in stride. Just like he handles everything else throughout his illness.

"Fine. You go ahead and do that."

Of course, I lost hours of sleep over that one sentence. How could I even begin to imagine a life without him? Never mind doing something that had been a bone of contention between us for years.

We never spoke about it again but it continues to haunt me.

This day, in the early years of our marriage, we are shopping with his mother and come across a pet store. I have always had a weakness for them. Every time I go in, I want to bring home as many critters as I can carry. My husband has literally pulled me from various establishments over the years. So I now try to avoid them.

Today, his mother wants to go so I relent and follow the two inside.

Immediately, my husband is drawn to an African Grey parrot. A half hour later, he has the parrot on his arm—and has fallen in love.

I have never been around birds before and don't see the attraction. But, being the forward-thinking type of person I am, I assume that if my husband gets a bird, then I will finally be able to get my dog.

"Okay," I say, after my husband has beseeched me over the $1,800 price tag. "I guess we can get a parrot."

That evening, my husband brings the parrot onto our bed. We have settled into the room for the night and are watching TV. Within seconds, the parrot walks over to me and roosts on my chest. I begin stroking her head—at the behest of my husband—and the parrot is soon cooing.

Okay. I think I can like birds, or at least this one.

Unfortunately, the parrot seems to be attracted to me more than my husband. And, apparently, they mate for life. Looks like I have become the chosen one; not necessarily what we had been looking for but I can certainly live with this.

Over the next few days and weeks, my husband tries everything under the sun to get the parrot to like him but still, the parrot refuses. She has become my pet. One day, I come home from a client meeting only to find my husband wearing my pajamas. After my fits of laughter subside, he explains that no, he is not a cross-dresser. He is only trying to persuade the parrot to spend time with him. But it doesn't work.

As the years pass, however, the parrot eventually transfers her affections from me to my husband. She finally becomes the pet that he always wanted. And it is with him that she makes her 'nest' when the feeling of motherhood arises. Although, it is me that ends up rushing her to the vet late one night after she begins making a series of choking sounds. Turns out, says the vet, that she was only laying an egg. Okay, I may have overreacted.

But regardless, for days after the egg laying, our parrot remains affixed to my husband's side.

African Greys are renowned for their ability to speak and there are many cases where they have extensive vocabularies of more than 1,000 words. At the time of purchase, our parrot already knew a few words, so we were quite excited about expanding her vocabulary.

Whenever the two of us travel, my mother faithfully comes to babysit the pets. She is always obliging and never seems to mind. What my mother doesn't fully understand, however, is my husband's tendency to swear—and to swear in techno-colour.

On one occasion, when the two of us are away at a press conference, I come across another Hungarian journalist. Excited that he is of the same nationality as my husband, I soon manoeuvre the two of them together.

"Say something in Hungarian," says the journalist, to my husband.

"I only know the swear words," my husband replies, with his wry grin.

"That's okay, go ahead," the journalist says.

At this point, I am basking in the glow of having orchestrated this intimate encounter.

My husband does as requested and utters a couple sentences. The next thing I know, the journalist spits his mouthful of wine all over me. He is nothing other than truly astonished at the potency of whatever my husband has just said.

"I did not expect you to speak quite like that," says the journalist, after apologizing for showering me with red wine. "This is something I have not heard before."

Needless to say, I never did find out what my husband had said, although he assured me it was quite graphic in detail.

Now that we have a potentially talking parrot, I insist that he be more mindful of these swear words. All we need is for the parrot to break into a stream of profanities while my mother is pet-sitting. That would put a quick end to our little travel jaunts. No doubt about it.

My husband agrees to be diligent and, for the most part, sticks to his word.

But we soon realize that there is no need.

Despite repeated attempts to extend our parrot's vocabulary, she refuses to speak. We buy DVDs. We go online to learn how to teach parrots to speak. We read books. We do everything that good parents should do. And still, she doesn't utter a word. In fact, the parrot soon loses the few words that she knew before joining our family.

We are obviously lacking somehow in the parent department. Good thing we never had kids.

The parrot does manage to learn, however, the meaning of certain words. She recognizes certain foods or events, like having a shower. It is not uncommon for either of us to be taking a shower only to have the water supply come to an abrupt stop. She has decided to join us and is hanging upside down from the showerhead, hogging the stream of hot water all to herself.

The parrot is also capable of mimicking whistles and other noises, and is able to repeat, note for note, my husband's whistling of the theme song to *The Bridge on the River Kwai*.

She also begins mimicking my husband's laugh.

And it is during these weeks and months afterwards, while I am lying in bed and slowly trying to get some semblance of a life back together, that she inevitably lets loose with his laugh. She laughs in the morning. At night. And whenever the mood strikes her. A constant reminder of who's missing.

Chapter Twenty-Nine

The time is passing slowly. And yet, still I ache for my husband. I see his favourite foods when I am out grocery shopping. I see his favourite TV shows broadcasting new episodes. I see the sun shining strong and think back to the dark winter when he died. How he would have loved to be here now, to enjoy all of these things.

My birthday comes around and I find myself once again immersed in a dark depression. My family tries to help but to no avail. And then his birthday arrives, and it gets even worse. These used to be special times. We would always celebrate privately, on our own, keeping these occasions reserved for just the two of us.

Our wedding anniversary arrives next.

"It's the 'firsts' of everything that are the worst," my sister advises. "Things will get easier once you get these 'firsts' behind you."

And then it's Christmas.

"I can't go," I say to my sister, the night before my father's annual Christmas get-together. "I can't do it. I'm not strong enough."

"Are you going to sit at home all alone instead?" she retorts. "How will that help? Come with us. We will pick you up and drop you off so you can have a few drinks. You will feel better for it. Trust me."

And so, I go. And it proves to be exactly the disaster I had predicted.

"I need to leave immediately," I whisper to my sister, now at her mercy, as I had acquiesced and gotten a ride with her and her family. "I can't do this any longer."

"Just give it a few more minutes," she responds. "The kids aren't finished opening their presents yet."

I had agonized over their presents this year, having to decide all on my own what to get them. It had always been something that the two of us did together. And I had cried as I wrote out the cards—my name the only one there.

"I am so sorry but I have to leave—now," I reply, the need to be out of that house and on my own overtaking me like a fever reaching its peak. I am getting exasperated and can literally no longer sit still. "I am going to start walking and you guys can catch up with me once you are on your way."

In desperation, I throw on my coat and head for the front door.

It is my nephew who drives me home shortly thereafter, before returning to the festivities.

"I am so sorry," he says, once we reach the safety of my front door. "We all miss him."

He gives me a hug that sets off my emotions once again. I stumble into the house as quickly as I can, trying to escape the humiliation of the evening.

Yes, time has passed. And, in some ways, I am getting stronger. But I soon realize that there are more hurdles that lie in wait ahead. I need to be stronger still, in order to overcome them.

And some of them are in my nightly dreams.

Where the dreams with my husband used to be full of car rides and adventures—all in good fun—they have now become ominous.

"I can't stay," my husband says to me one night.

I am so joyful to see him again that it takes a moment for the words to sink in.

"What do you mean? You can't stay where? The house? This room?" I ask, feeling my anxiety increase.

"No. It's not the house. It's you. I can't stay with you," he replies. "I've met someone else."

"What?" I ask incredulously. "You've actually met someone else? You're leaving me? But how can you? I don't believe you."

"There is no explanation," he replies. "I have met somebody else. Our marriage has been over for a long time now. You know that. There is no point in staying together anymore."

I am emotionally crushed. To experience the sheer joy of seeing him again, after thinking he has been dead all of these months. Only for him to tell me that he no longer wants to be with me. It just doesn't sink in.

Years ago, we had been at a press event and there was a fortune teller on-site. I had, for the fun of it, stopped to have my palm read.

"Your marriage will not last," she said at the time.

I was flabbergasted.

"There is no way that I will be getting a divorce," I emphatically stated. "You are so wrong."

"It may not end in divorce," she said, as I angrily got up to leave. "Marriages do end in other ways."

I knew that she was wrong but still remembered the encounter all of these years later. It now seems that she had been right after all.

"Is that why you've been away?" I ask my husband again. "Is that why you led me to believe that you were dead? All of this time you've been gone and now you tell me that you've met somebody else. How can you be so cruel?"

And then I awake.

But instead of the warm and fuzzy feeling of being wrapped in a cocoon of happiness from my dreams of before, I am upset and saddened. My husband wants to leave me. I know now that it's just a dream but it's painful nonetheless.

Why is he doing this? It would have been better if he had just stayed away and let me go on thinking he was dead.

Another night and we're at it again.

"I've been away because you need to realize that it's over between us," he says, frustrated with my constant barrage of questions. "We're over. We're through. There is no more 'us'."

"But I am so happy to see you. I don't understand. How can you do this to us? How can you give up?"

But there is no point. In my dreams (nightmares, I suppose you could call them), he is forever telling me that we're through. That our marriage is in shambles; that it's over.

What has proven to be one of my greatest escapes in this whole ordeal has been brutally yanked away from me. How will I cope now?

"How did you get through this?" I ask my husband's best friend one day. He had lost his wife to cancer several years earlier. "How do you go on?"

"You just do it," he replies. "You have no choice but to do it."

I remember that same friend telling me that one day, something will happen that will make me smile. And when that happens, he said, that's the start of a new path forward.

It is weeks after my sister's and my trip to Berlin when I am at home, looking out the window, and spot a stray cat with her four kittens. They are playing in the yard beside the house—clearly visible from our bank of large windows. I think back to our own cat and her litter of kittens. Of how much joy they had brought us and I can't help but smile. I think of my husband's friend then and I thank him for his prescient words.

In the following days and weeks, I leave food for the cat and her litter. The kittens grow big and strong, and eventually, they leave to find their own way in the world. And I actually feel joy at having had the privilege of watching over them.

Things change.

I guess that's one of the hardest things about losing someone. Things change. I automatically reach for the phone or make a mental note about what I have to tell my husband. Even after all of these months, he is still very much a part of me.

And I know now that he will always remain a part of me. And that, in a way, provides some solace. Sure, I still have days when I am mad at the world, mad at him for leaving me. But I also have other days when I am okay, when I can venture out on my own or when I can, once again, visit with friends.

The emotional day-to-day gains seem excruciatingly infinitesimal but eventually, all these tiny steps become cumulative. And, as the months pass, I feel myself getting stronger and stronger. Business picks up and before I know it, I am working long hours again. But more important, I am almost to the point where I can think back and be happy for the time we've had together, instead of feeling angry for the time we didn't.

"You have come a long way," says my mother one day, while we are out on our weekly movie date. This is a mother-daughter tradition that started early into the grieving process, enabling both of us to lose ourselves in someone else's reality for a couple of hours at a time. "I'm proud of you."

My mother has ended up being a strength to me after all. Despite whatever happened between her and my father—and the many acrimonious years since—she has been steadfast in her support. And she is quick to remind me that the years I did have with my husband were better than most people's.

"You two had a very special relationship," she says. "Those kinds of partnerships come along only once in a lifetime—if that. You're so lucky to have had that wonderful experience."

I know she is thinking back to her own failed marriage with my father and to the many unsettled years since. And as much as I agree that I was fortunate enough to have experienced a truly wonderful and mutually loving relationship, there is still part of me that questions why it had to end. What crime or misdemeanor did we do to deserve this? I guess that old, Catholic upbringing never does quite go away.

My search for words of advice from my husband is over. I have rifled through the house from top to bottom and failed to turn up anything. I'm forced instead to aimlessly peruse old photos, videos and memories.

"You're still young," my husband says to me, a couple of years into his diagnosis, when we both know there is no cure in sight. "You'll find someone else."

"Oh, I don't think so," I reply. We are in his car on one of our lovely jaunts into the countryside, going nowhere fast and enjoying every minute of it. "I think you're the one."

"Well," he says. "When you're with 'the two', I want you to be happy. I want you to get over me and get on with your life."

"I don't want to," I retort. "I don't want to lose you."

I remember again the wise words of the friend on how he coped with losing his wife, how he got through the whole sickness part only to lose her. "You just do it."

The phrase pretty much sums it up. You take one moment at a time and aim to get through it. The alternative is to give in and down a fistful of pills. As alluring as that may be, the desire to do so does tend to ebb in time. It does get easier.

One day, I take all of the assorted pill bottles that I have hoarded over this past year and drop them off at the local pharmacy. I don't need that safety net anymore. I am stronger today than I was yesterday, and I will be even stronger tomorrow.

But I am not strong right now. I am in the veterinarian's office with my cat.

"She is a sick, little kitty," says the vet. This is after numerous blood tests and x-rays that reveal congestive heart failure and asthma, along with something in her lungs that could or could not be scar tissue. More than likely, it's a slow-growing type of tumour of some sort. But she won't survive an operation.

I go home in a daze. The wall of grief has descended once again—as quickly and as darkly as its predecessor. I can't cope. I can't go through this. This was his little cat, the apple of his eye. She helped him get through those endless days of sickness and poor health. She was his rock. But since he died, this cat has been my steadfast companion. She has become my rock. And I am not willing to give her up.

"My husband's dog died last week," says a lady to me while at the hospital one day. My husband and I have come to know her over these past few months. Her husband has the same disease and has sort of been the 'guinea pig' for new

111

treatments. My husband and I have often turned to him for advice or insight on what to expect. It's strange how quickly friendships form in the most unlikely places. But the treatments that proved somewhat successful for him didn't have the same results for us. He died a month before my husband, after an 11-year struggle with the disease.

"I can't believe that the universe would be so cruel as to take away his best friend at a time like this," says his wife, who would become an e-mail pal of mine for years to come. "To have to cope with the finality of this disease and then to have this happen now, when he is so close to the end. I just can't believe that someone would let this happen."

Fortunately, our little kitty made it through my husband's illness—soon to become the rock that would ground me through my journey of despair. I wasn't ready to lose her.

"Your husband wants her back," says my mother, when I finally am coherent enough to call her on the phone. "He's let you have her for a while. But now he wants her with him."

"Well," I say defiantly, "he can't have her. I will fight him with everything I can."

And so begins, round after round of medication and treatment. And although she may not be getting better, she is not getting worse.

Chapter Thirty

I have let many old friends and acquaintances drift away over these past few years—mainly because of my own overriding need to withdraw inward. But some do remain.

Slowly, I begin re-integrating into society. It starts with meeting one old friend for dinner and then another. I realize that the friendships still remain, despite the long bouts of silence that often ensue. These are people with whom my husband and I once socialized, and interacted with on a regular basis. But as much as I still enjoy their company and appreciate the times we've had together, I cherish those times when no one knows my story. When I can put on my façade and pretend to be just like everybody else.

I find myself drifting to those friends who were more mine than my husband's or even ours. The ones I used to go running with or take dance lessons with. The girlfriends that every female half of a couple continues to have, even after marriage has changed the landscape.

It is these female friends in whom I now find solace and it is through weekly dinners or get-togethers that I begin to build up the confidence needed for being alone. Sure, there are moments when I will talk of the past—something I would have been incapable of just months before—but there are new memories to build. These girlfriends offer me a safe environment in which I can re-learn what it means to be just me, alone. It's been more than 20 years since I have been on my own and figuring out how to do it again has proven to be a long and arduous process.

It is one of these girlfriends who convinces me to join the local YMCA. Always a bit of a fitness fanatic, I have been swimming or running my way through these turbulent years.

"Maybe it's time to shake things up," she says one day, advising me to meet her for a fitness class that evening.

And so begins the shaping of a new world for me. This is the re-born me, the one where I appear on the scene as a strong, independent person. No one here knows my story, and the level of socializing that occurs before and after these fitness classes pretty much guarantees that I don't have to reveal my story to anyone unless I want to. It's another new and safe environment, and one that I take to like a fish takes to water.

Within a few weeks, I have become addicted to my new routine. I work out in the mornings when I can and then do my freelance work in the afternoon. It's the perfect scenario for me at this particular moment in time. And it remains so for months to come.

Until one day, I confide a little bit of my story to one of the instructors. I still don't understand how it happened, why I decided to open up a teeny-weeny bit. I had always clammed up and changed the subject whenever anything personal came up in conversation. Sure, I could answer the trite: "Do you have any children?"

"No. You?"

"Are you married?"

"Was. You?"

"Where do you live?"

"Not far. What about you?"

Always answer a question with a question and you'd be amazed at how little you can end up revealing about yourself.

This day, after months of seeing the same people day in and day out, turns out to be different from the others, and when the instructor begins talking about her life, and some of the difficulties she has undergone recently, I inadvertently chime in and do a small reveal.

"My husband died a couple years ago."

"I'm so sorry. How did he die?"

"Cancer."

And thus, the wall of silence is finally broken. And little by little, as the days progress, I let out a bit more. It will prove to be some time yet before I can be as candid as I'd like but still, I've made a huge leap forward. And I am still standing.

It is during this time that I also begin venturing back to the neighbours. They lived next door to us for about eight years, had gotten to know me and my husband quite well. We often went over to their place for dinner and then had them over to ours. Being out in the country meant that neither of us was too intrusive. We respected each other's space—and privacy.

I had ceased communication right after the diagnosis, other than a quick email explaining the situation with the barest of facts.

The neighbours had tried maintaining contact with me but soon realized that contact was the last thing I wanted. They respectfully kept their distance until the memorial. We had re-connected then but had gone back to the new-old routine right after.

Until I answered the phone one day.

"Come for dinner. We so want to see you. It's been way too long."

And so, I went. I just grabbed the house key, locked the door and walked over.

Of course, I broke down in tears as soon as I saw them. But hugs were plentiful—as was the wine—and I did manage to stay for a couple hours.

Soon after, the visits became part of my new routine. Every Friday night, we would get together for wine and potato chips. Always at their place. Never at ours—or mine as it now was. No, our house was still our sanctuary and I would protect it at all costs.

Until I awoke one morning and realized that I couldn't live there anymore. It was time to move on. As much as I loved the house and found it a comfort in every way possible, I had reached the point where I could no longer stay.

There were countless memories there, but I knew now that I could take them with me wherever I went. The fact was that it was out in the middle of nowhere, and it was a century-old home that required a ton of maintenance. I was nowhere near to being up to the task. My idea of gardening was to hire someone to do it.

Since my husband died, I had hired a pool serviceman, a gardener, a window cleaner, a yard man, a handy man—you name it, I hired it. And it was proving to be expensive.

I began venturing out on drives again—something my husband and I used to do together so long ago. But this time, I was checking out the little towns and villages in the surrounding area. I needed to move—of that I was sure—but to where was still up in the air.

Until I found a little village near the lake. It was a new subdivision in an old town that had been given a new lease on life. There were the basic amenities: a liquor store, grocery store, pizza place, etc. Nothing like what was available in the nearby cities but more than enough for me. It was people and activity that I now craved, having spent months and months in loneliness and despair.

A visit to the builder's office informed me that the developer was currently sold out but was taking registrations for the next phase.

"However," says the sales lady, "we do have a couple of houses that are available. The builder let the original buyers out of their contracts. The only caveat is that houses are already finished so they can't be customized."

Sounds like a good deal to me.

And as soon as I walked into the first of the two, I knew instantly that this is where I needed to be.

A visit to the bank and the real estate agent set things in motion. I actually bought the new house before even putting my own up for sale. But it all worked out in the end.

In May of that year, three years after my husband died, I set out on a new path forward by moving into my brand new home.

Of course, my sister was on hand to help, as were my mother and father.

"I'm glad to know that you're no longer living out in the country on your own," confides my father, when we finally stop in exhaustion during the move and are sitting in the kitchen of my new house, eating pizza. "I won't have to worry about you quite as much now."

Once a father, always a father. Okay, he may not be perfect. But he is still my dad.

My mother proves her worth in gold as well, working just as diligently as the rest of us as we unpack. She and I have spent weeks beforehand furniture shopping, and we both wait in anticipation of what the final outcome will be.

And we aren't disappointed.

And thus begins another new chapter of my life. I have gone through hell and back but I am finally at a point where I can honestly say that I am content. I am not nearly as happy as I was before but not nearly as unhappy either. That's something to be proud of, isn't it?

Chapter Thirty-One

It's been four years now since my husband has died. I believe that I have travelled a great distance during this time. I have made it through the dark chasm of pain that surrounded me for months on end and have emerged, somewhat tentatively, on the other side. I have acquired a new outlook on life that borders on the realm of optimistic. And I still have my cat.

The move has proven to be a wise choice, and I am just as happy when I open the front door and step inside my new home as I was on the very day I moved in. Yes, it's taken a lot, emotionally and physically, to make it mine. But I do love it. And, in its own way, it's become a new sanctuary for me.

Every once in a while, I drive past the old house where my husband and I used to live. The new owner has made small changes but you can tell that he cares about it. That's all I ask. That the new owner loves that house as much as my husband and I did. We had many happy times there—more than 20 years together in blissful solitude.

It's a sad remembrance but a happy one at the same time. I guess I have progressed, at least a bit.

Today, I am accompanying my mother and father—the two have since left their respective partners and are once again on speaking terms—to another hospital to talk to another doctor. As soon as I walk through the doors, I am met with a tidal wave of emotions and memories. It's strange how one hospital is so like any other. My first instinct is to run back and wait in the car. My second is to offer support to my parents.

"I'm sorry to say that there is no cure," the oncologist says, looking at my father. "The prostate cancer that you had years ago has metastasized into bone cancer. It's a slow-progressing disease that we will treat for as long as we can."

My mother and father don't say anything. They turn towards me.

Unfortunately, I know the drill. I've been here before. I can do this again. I know I can.